About the Author

Kieran Larwood has loved fantasy stories since reading *The Hobbit* as a boy. He graduated from Southampton University with a degree in English Literature and then worked as a Reception class teacher for fifteen years. He has just about recovered. He now writes full-time although, if anybody was watching, they might think he just daydreams a lot and drinks too much coffee.

About the Illustrator

David Wyatt lives in Devon. He has illustrated many novels but is also much admired for his concept and character work. He has illustrated tales by a number of high-profile fantasy authors such as Diana Wynne Jones, Terry Pratchett, Philip Pullman and J. R. R. Tolkien.

The Five Realms series

The Five Realms

Uki
and the
Swamp Spirit

Kieran Larwood

Illustrated by David Wyatt

faber

First published in 2020
by Faber & Faber Limited
Bloomsbury House,
74–77 Great Russell Street,
London WC1B 3DA
faberchildrens.co.uk
This paperback edition first published in 2021

Typeset in Times by M Rules
Printed by CPI Group (UK) Ltd, Croydon CR0 4YY
All rights reserved
Text, map pp.viii-ix, illustrations pp.337-338 and chapter head illustrations
© Kieran Larwood, 2020
Illustrations © David Wyatt, 2020

A CIP record for this book
is available from the British Library

ISBN 978–0–571–34283–9

2 4 6 8 10 9 7 5 3 1

To Claire

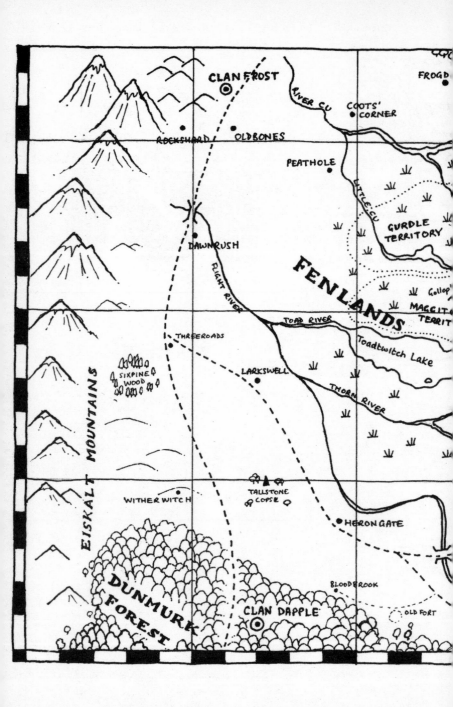

ALL

TOCK

WIC

NIGHTEYE CHINE

BLACKSAND BAY

BADLUCK BEACH

BLOODTHORN
(CLAN SHRIKE)

ISLE OF
THORNS

EELBURY

ENK

THE MOUTH

WRAITHSTONE
RUINS

GREAT
EPING

SMUGGLERS'
BLUFF

HEN
TARN

Central

Hulstland

ENDLESS SEA

Prologue

The buzzard leaps from his perch on the barren treetop and heaves himself into the sky with *whooshing* beats of his wings. He catches a thermal at the edge of the forest and rides it upwards, circling, drifting like a plank of wood on a lazy ocean current.

Down below is a scrubland of matted grass where the trees end – a good source of mice and voles. His needle-sharp eyes jump here and there, hunting for signs of twitches and scurries. He daydreams of furry treats, full of hot blood and meat.

Gliding, watching, he passes over the tumbles of

stone things. Normally cold and empty, they have an aura he doesn't like. A death-feeling. Somewhere to keep away from. There's never any prey there, anyway. Not even a scrawny mouse.

So he's surprised to see rabbits. Five of them, running around the ruins.

Despite the chill it gives his feathers, he circles lower, watching the figures as they dash about. Somewhere, deep in the back of his ancient bird-memories, he remembers rabbits as food. It makes his talons prickle and he flexes them ... but that was many thousands of years ago. These are man-rabbits. Not the fluffy little parcels of lunch from the days of his fathers and mothers before. These ones walk on two legs. They have flying claws that can *swish* up at you, even if you're in the air. They shout and throw stones if you get too near. Dangerous, unpredictable creatures.

Still, sometimes they drop things you can eat. Or, even better, they fight each other and leave dead ones on the ground. Then, if you're quick, you can swoop down and snatch a juicy eyeball or tongue before they chase you off.

The buzzard circles some more, just in case one of the rabbits drops dead.

He has no such luck. Three of them hide behind piles of bricks and start yelling, firing off their claws at something in the old tower. The other two run away from the cold, stone place to where there are some giant rats, tied up behind a cluster of bramble bushes. They jump on their backs and ride off; one to the south, the other east, across the mountains.

The buzzard follows them, drifting above, hoping something tasty might drop from a pack or satchel. But nothing does, and soon the man-rabbits are gone.

There is nothing to eat here, and all that shouting has scared the prey away.

Stupid, noisy creatures. The buzzard beats its wings, skims the clouds and heads off over the forest, in hopes of a squirrel or two for lunch.

CHAPTER ONE

The Night-Sparrow

'Are they still there?'

Jori puts an eye to the gap in the rubble and is rewarded by the *zing* of an arrow. It smacks against the stonework with a bang, sending up sparks and making her jerk back inside the tower.

'Yes, Rue,' she says. 'I think it's safe to say they are.'

The little rabbit sighs. They have been stuck inside the ruins of Doomgate, the old Endwatch tower, all day now. They had thought the place deserted when they arrived, but a band of armed

6

Endwatch agents were occupying it, and now have them trapped inside the stone hulk. There is no way to escape without being shot. Which meant hours of silence, with nothing to do except watch a patch of sunlight move across the dusty floor.

The bard is still standing by the collection of parchment prophecies on the wall, tugging his beard and looking worried. Jori, the scarred ex-assassin in her patched armour, has searched the whole place from top to bottom several times, looking for a route out. Rue has counted the pale white tendrils of sun-starved plants creeping up the walls. He has drawn patterns and spirals in the gritty dirt on the floor; had a nap or two, curled in his cloak; played a pretend game of Neekball with some rocks for jerboas and a curled-up pillbug for the ball. He has even quietly sung a few songs to his little sparrow as it hopped about its cage.

Being trapped by enemies is extremely *boring*.

'I'm going to search the library again, before it gets dark,' says Jori. 'There might be an opening I've missed. Coming, Rue?'

Rue shakes his head. He's been down there once,

but something about that dim, musty place gives him the creeps. Softly glowing mushrooms cover the far wall, where damp has got in. There are stacks of crumbling scrolls and parchment everywhere. All those ancient stories, all that ghostly knowledge of centuries past, silent and mouldering ...

'Can we eat soon?' he asks. 'My tummy is rumbling.'

'When I get back,' says Jori. She takes a candle and heads over to the open trapdoor, lighting the wick with a flint. She pauses to check the silver-capped bottle of dusk potion on her belt before climbing down the ladder.

Over by the wall, the bard is still deep in thought. Rue thinks about asking him a question or two, but decides against it. Instead he listens to the bumps and scrapes of Jori searching below, keeping one eye on the gap in the rubble in case an Endwatch rabbit with a bow or spear should suddenly pop through. He always feels much safer when Jori is right beside him. Who wouldn't, with one of the best fighters in the Five Realms as their bodyguard?

Eventually she comes back, shaking her head

and looking glum. 'Nothing,' she says. 'No way out except this hole in the rubble, here.'

'So we really are absolutely, completely, properly trapped,' says Rue.

'I'm afraid so. Let's take our minds off it with some dinner.'

Rummaging in the packs, Jori brings out a hunk of flatbread and a handful of pumpkin seeds. She shares it into three piles.

'We'd better ration the food,' she says. 'We don't know how long we'll be stuck here.'

'Master?' Rue calls to the bard, who replies with a grunt. 'Master, will you come and eat?'

Still tugging his beard, the bard wanders over. He perches on a toppled piece of stonework and picks up his pile of bread and seeds. Rue watches the bard eat as he nibbles at his own handful, waiting for him to say something, but he doesn't. He looks as worried as Rue has seen him, since becoming his apprentice last spring.

The tiny dinner is soon gone. Rue saves some seeds to feed the little sparrow in its cage.

'Better give that bird a few more.' The bard finally

breaks his silence. 'We'll be needing him to take a message to Gant back in Melt.'

Rue remembers the kindly Foxguard agent they had stayed with. 'Now?' he asks. The thought of the little bird leaving makes him sad. Its cheerful fluttering has been the only thing comforting him all day.

'Soon,' says the bard. 'When it's dark. Don't want those villains shooting it down. Then we really will be trapped.'

'Will Gant send help?' Rue asks. 'How long before they arrive?'

'That depends on how fast the bird is,' says Jori. She pours a pile of seeds into its cage. 'If it flies all night, it might make it there by morning. Then if Gant sends Jaxom and his jerboas right away, they could get here with two days' hard riding.'

'I'd say it's going to be at least three,' says the bard. 'He'll have to find Jaxom, maybe get some more armed rabbits to come with him. And we need him to raise the Foxguard first. The Endwatch must be stopped. That's more important.'

'Is this about what they're going to do to Podkin?'

Rue has been *itching* to ask all day. 'You said he was hiding in Thornwood, but that can't be true. Thornwood is *my* warren, and I've never seen him.'

'You didn't see him because he didn't want to be seen,' says the bard. 'But he was there all the same.'

'You mean I've actually been near the real, actual, living, *actual* Podkin One-Ear? The hero who defeated the Gorm? The legend who collected the Goddess's Gifts?'

'All your life,' says the bard. For the first time that long, long day he smiles.

'But who is he? The fat doorman? Mistletoe the cook? One of my father's servants?'

'Nobody you would have noticed,' says the bard. 'Just an old longbeard, sitting by the fire.'

'An old rabbit? Is that all?' Rue can hardly believe it. 'But how can *Podkin* not be noticed? Doesn't greatness shine out of his eyes? Can't you hear the power when he speaks? Doesn't he ... *smell* like a legend?'

The bard chuckles. 'He's just an ordinary rabbit, like the rest of us, I'm afraid. When you're as old as us, nothing shines out of your eyes any more.

And you don't smell of anything much except old turnips.'

'But if he's just an elderly, harmless rabbit, why do the Endwatch want to kill him? How do they even know about him? Aren't they part of *Uki*'s story? Podkin's enemies were the Gorm . . .'

The bard's green eyes glint with tears, and Rue remembers that Podkin is the bard's brother, and he must be worried about him. 'It's all part of the same tale,' says the bard. 'And to understand you have to hear it all. Then you will know the danger we face.'

'Well, then,' says Rue, with the glee of a hunter who has just sprung his trap, 'what are we waiting for? I want to hear about how Uki captured the other spirits. Which one came after Valkus? And what does it all have to do with Podkin?'

'Later, later,' says the bard. 'Let's get this sparrow flying, and then see if we can survive until morning. I bet those Endwatch scum try something in the night.'

'We will have to set a watch,' says Jori. She rummages in her pack and brings out a little wooden box. Inside is ink, a pen and some thin slivers of parchment. 'Get your message written now, though.

The quicker we send the bird, the quicker help might come.'

The bard takes some parchment and begins to write on it in minute letters. Rue peers over his shoulder, trying to read them, but they are in Hulst runes rather than Ogham. He has no idea what they say. Hopefully something along the lines of: WE ARE ABOUT TO DIE. SEND HELP IMMEDIATELY. AN ARMY WOULD BE GOOD. HURRY, HURRY, HURRY.

The bard rolls the parchment into a tiny scroll and then fishes the sparrow from its cage and holds it gently while Jori ties the message to its leg. Then they pop it back for a feast of pumpkin seeds and wait for night to fall.

*

The dark comes quickly in this part of the world. Soon the ruined tower room is pitch-black, with a chill that seeps up from the floor and crawls into your bones. Somehow, they resist the urge to light a fire, or even a candle. Rue cuddles up next to the bard for warmth, the sparrow's cage on his lap. He wishes he had wings too, so he could fly away from this cold, lonely place.

'I reckon it's dark enough,' says Jori. She is perched on the rubble pile that blocks the doorway, peering out through the hole at the top. 'The Endwatch have lit a fire somewhere. Probably cooking dinner and keeping warm. The glare will make it harder for them to see.'

'Could we slip out too, do you think?' Rue asks. 'Jori could take her dusk potion and chop them all to pieces in the dark.'

'I appreciate your confidence in me,' says Jori, with a little smile. 'But it would be too risky. They might not see a tiny sparrow, but they'll definitely see us. Not to mention hear us breaking our way through these bricks. And I might be fast with the potion, but I'm not faster than an arrow.'

'It's something we might have to consider, though,' says the bard. 'Once our food and water are gone.'

There's a moment of silence as they all ponder that terrible thought. Then the bard takes the sparrow cage from Rue and gently lifts the bird out.

'Goodbye, little one,' Rue whispers. 'And good luck.'

'Good luck indeed,' says the bard. He passes the bird to Jori, who gently raises it to the gap in the rubble with cupped hands. With a last peek to make sure the Endwatch are still busy, she lets the bird fly.

They all hold their breath as it flutters upwards, waiting for an arrow to come streaking and smash it into a puff of feathers.

None does, thank the Goddess, and soon the little bird is lost in the darkness.

The bard lets out his breath in a whoosh. 'Clarion's bongos, that was tense. Now, do you think we can build ourselves a fire? There's enough bits of old table and bench in here to burn.'

Working together, they build a small ring of stones and fill it with wood and kindling. It burns well, and although it makes the room smoky, the light and warmth are very welcome.

'I'll take first watch,' says Jori. 'I'll wake you in a few hours.'

The bard nods and rolls himself up in his cloak. Rue is about to protest and ask for a story, but discovers that his eyes are extremely heavy. All the terror and worry of the day has worn him out, and soon he is falling asleep too, listening to the crackle of the fire and pretending he is home at Thornwood, playing a game of fox paw with Podkin himself.

*

The smell of toasted bread and blackberry tea wakes him, and for a moment Rue thinks his mother is about to call him for breakfast. He jumps up, ready to fight his many brothers for a portion, only to find he is still in the dingy tower room, the air thick with smoke and the gleam of dawn sunlight streaking through the rubble-choked doorway.

Jori is at the fireside, pouring tea from a copper kettle into three clay cups. She smiles when she sees him wake, and places his tea beside him. The bard is sitting on the heap of broken bricks and timber that used to be the entrance, peering out of the hole at the top.

'Those mangy dog-weasels are up and about,' he mutters. 'I can see their campfire smoking.'

As if in answer, a voice shouts from outside. 'Enjoy your breakfast! It might be your last! We have more rabbits on the way. You don't stand a chance!'

'That's funny,' the bard shouts back. 'While you lot were twiddling your ears and snoozing, we sent a sparrow for help. There'll be a whole platoon of angry Foxguard here before you know it. Then we'll see how tough you are!'

The Endwatch let fly an arrow, which pings off the stone doorway. Then there is silence.

'That's got the wind up them,' the bard chuckles. 'They won't be so cocky now.'

'Probably shouldn't have told them about the sparrow,' says Jori. 'Now they'll be on their guard.'

The bard's ears droop. 'Sorry,' he says. 'Didn't think of that.'

'Are more Endwatch really coming?' Rue asks. 'Will they get here before Jaxom does?'

'Morning, Rue,' says the bard. He clambers down from the doorway and walks over to ruffle the young rabbit's ears. 'Don't you worry. They were just trying to scare us.'

Jori nods. 'Yes, don't worry. I don't expect there's more than those five Endwatchers in the whole of Hulstland.'

'And if there are any others, they wouldn't waste

17

their time trying to get us. Not when there are more important carrots to peel.'

'Podkin, you mean?' Rue sips his tea. It's warm and sweet, but it doesn't stop the chill that has crept through him in the night. His paws shake as he holds the cup.

'Yes,' says the bard. He watches Rue with worried eyes for a long moment. 'Listen, little one, you don't need to be so scared. Everything is going to be all right. We'll be out of here before you know it, and I've told Gant to warn the rest of the Foxguard. They'll be able to protect Podkin and everyone in Thornwood warren. Besides, your father and his warriors will be more than a match for the Endwatch. I'd like to see anyone get past Hubert the Broad when his fur is ruffled.'

'But we could be here for *days*,' says Rue. He is overcome with a wave of homesickness, stronger than any he has felt since leaving last spring. The dreams of his mother, the talk of Thornwood ... suddenly it is all too much and his eyes fill with tears. 'I want to go *home*. I want my mother,' he sobs.

The bard reaches across and pulls him into a hug.

They sit for a while, quietly rocking back and forth as the fire crackles and the smoke swirls in the sunlight.

'I tell you what,' says the bard. 'We've got a lot of time on our paws. Why don't I tell you the rest of Uki's story? That should take your mind off things.'

'Yes, please,' says Rue, from somewhere in the folds of the bard's cloak.

'Good idea,' says Jori. 'I'd especially like to hear about his brave and heroic companion. She was the best part of the tale.'

'You mean Kree, the little plains rabbit?' says the bard, knowing full well she meant herself, and then chuckles as Jori throws a chunk of toasted bread at him.

With Rue still snuggled up in his cloak, the bard clears his throat and begins to speak . . .

CHAPTER Two

The Evening Count

The good thing about stories, Rue – or rather, *one* of the good things – is that, if you're feeling sad, or worried, or lonely ... or if, like us, you're trapped in a ruined tower by a bunch of murderous villains ... they can take your mind off things. Stories can lift you out of the unpleasant real world and off into another. Even if it's just for a few moments. And when you come back to your own personal story ... well, things don't usually seem as bad.

That's another reason why us bards are so

important. We help people sidestep life for a bit. And you never know … hearing about some brave, determined, heroic little rabbits might help you find that part of yourself.

Because it's there, in all of us.

('Even me?' Rue whispers.

'Especially you,' Jori whispers back.)

Talking of heroes: I recall we left Uki running from the smouldering battleground of Syn and Nys, the twin cities of Northern Hulstland. Singed and bedraggled, he had managed to escape in one piece – with Jori and Kree, but there was no time to celebrate their victory. Their quest was only half done.

It had just been a few months earlier that Uki had been cast out of his tribe because his eyes and fur were coloured differently on either side. The Ice Waste rabbits had thought him a demon. A bad omen. Weak and starving, his mother dead, he had been brought back from the brink of death by bonding with an ancient spirit named Iffrit. Iffrit had once been the guardian of four other spirits, who had escaped from him. He now gave Uki all his power and tasked him with recapturing them, using shards of the crystal prison they had once been sealed in. Two spirits had now been caught, trapped in glowing gems on Uki's spear harness. The special powers they gave him pulsed through his blood, making Uki the strongest little rabbit in all the Five Realms. But these powers would only become permanent if Uki managed to locate all four. If he didn't succeed, the spirits would run riot again, gaining power and taking over the whole rabbit world, while Iffrit's magic would fade away, along with Uki himself.

To complicate things, the witch Necripha and her servant Balto were on their tail. Leaders of the Endwatch, they wanted the powers of the spirits for themselves. Their sinister network of agents was everywhere, watching and plotting from the shadows. And to make matters worse, there was a good chance that Jori's evil cousin, Venic, might be following them too. He wanted to hand Jori back to her family, to be punished for refusing to become an assassin. He was also probably quite miffed at Uki for throwing him into a wall.

All this weighed heavy on the young rabbits' minds. The challenge ahead of them was terrifying.

Still, they allowed themselves a brief stop to lick their wounds and wash the smoke from their clothes before pressing on. Uki could tell where the other spirits were. Their presence was like fish hooks in his brain – a constant, gentle tugging – as if a sleepy angler snoozed on a distant riverbank, with the line tied to his toe.

The closest was due south, and the other further off to the west. Both would have travelled inside the bodies of Nurg's poor brothers. Both would probably have shed their simple hosts and wormed their way into rabbits of power and strength, just as Valkus had. But they would have had more time to make themselves at home. And both would do anything they could to avoid being captured inside Uki's crystals.

Keeping the waves of the Endless Sea to their left, the rabbits headed along the coast, crossing the bridge over the Bleak River, and taking the road that skirted the cluster of pine and spruce trees known as the Coldwood.

Here, Jori got especially nervous, as her clan warren was based nearby. Even though it was over a day's walk away, at the north-western edge of the wood, her clanmates often roamed the trees, foraging for dusk angel mushrooms, which they brewed into the highly poisonous dusk potion that gave their warriors such incredible speed. They would know that Jori had run away from the clan. They would be ready to capture her, or worse. The last thing she wanted was to bump into one.

'Relax,' Kree said to her. 'Even if they do spot us, Uki can throw them all the way back to Melt. He has the strength of a god, you know.'

Of a god. Uki looked down at his skinny little arms. It was bizarre to think that they flowed with the power of Iffrit, Gaunch and now Valkus. But he could feel it tingling there. If he wanted to, he could pull up a tree by the roots and bash any rabbit of Clan Septys they found over the head. He could . . .

'It doesn't matter how strong he is,' Jori said, interrupting his thoughts. 'A dusk wraith like me could fill him full of poison darts before he even took a breath. He wouldn't be able to throw a pebble if his bones were all melted and his muscles turned to jelly.'

As one, they pulled their hoods low and hurried

along in silence, praying they reached the other side undetected.

They now sat on a high, gorse-spotted hill, munching a simple lunch and looking down at the landscape before them. Uki marvelled at how the world had completely changed again. The wide, red-tinged Blood Plains had seemed so strange to him, having lived all his life in the bleak Ice Wastes. Now he saw miles of low swampland, stretching off to the horizon ... a network of winding lakes and rivers, like a maze, and in between were seas of reeds, clusters of trees and the odd little hummock sticking up like an anthill. There were shades of green, yellow and brown everywhere, and the patches of water sparked sunbeams like diamonds.

Off to the west, along the same stretch of hillside they stood on, was a cluster of earth mounds, ringed by a high stone wall. Thin trails of smoke trickled up into the air from hidden chimneys. There was a similar walled enclosure in the valley below, and one far ahead in the distance, at the very edge of the reeds and marshes.

'The Fenlands,' said Jori, sweeping her arm across

the view. 'A den of backward savages, bandits and smugglers. Nothing has changed here for a hundred years and probably won't for another hundred.'

'Are those warrens?' Uki asked, pointing at the walled group of mounds.

'Yes,' said Jori. 'Rabbits on the edge of the marshes don't live in buildings like up north, and don't quite live underground like the southerners. They cover their stone houses with turf and then wall them in for safety. That's Frogdeep Hall on the hillside. The warren at the bottom of the hill is Mudstock, and the one on the edge of the fen is Reedwic.'

'What about that wet, gloopy place with all the rivers?' Kree asked. 'Do rabbits live there?'

'They do,' said Jori. 'And those are the most backward ones of all. They don't like outsiders. In fact, I've never seen one. I've heard stories, though. About savages dressed in frogskin who worship toads and eels. Please don't tell me that's where we have to go.'

'Do your thing, Uki,' said Kree. 'Find the spirit for us, with your thoughts.'

Uki's connection to the escaped spirits meant he could sense things about them – where they were, what they were feeling. It sometimes came to him in visions, or when he focused his mind on them. But it was a horrible, draining thing to do. And seeing through the eyes of such ancient, terrible evil . . . he had been trying to put it off since they left Syn.

Now there was no excuse for delay. He gave a deep sigh and then closed his eyes, reaching out for that invisible thread joining him to the spirit, pulling himself along it to the source.

The first thing he felt was life.

Masses of it. The fen was seething and pulsing with creeping, slithering, buzzing, flapping, stalking creatures. Not like the Ice Wastes, or even the plains, where animals struggled to scrape by in the unforgiving cold. Here it was warm and fertile and teeming. If he scooped up a pawful of water, he knew it would be thronged with hordes of living beasties, some even smaller than he could see.

It took his breath away for a moment and he wondered how he could be sensing it all. Then he realised it was because of the spirit itself. *There,* right in the heart of the fen, was his target. It oozed and throbbed and Uki had the sensation of a sickly green light, spreading out through the networks of water. Of tendrils connecting all the creatures of the marsh in a web. Seeking them, joining them . . . *changing* them. He could feel the life, because the spirit was linking itself to it. Linking itself so it could poison it all and destroy it.

Uki was filled with a sudden rush of sickness. He could taste bile at the back of his throat, feel his joints begin to swell and ache, his blood thicken and turn bad.

Charice. The name came to him from the fragments of memory that Iffrit had left in his head. Charice was one of the four spirits that Iffrit had watched over in the crystal prison buried deep beneath the earth for thousands and thousands of years. Like the others, she had been created by the Ancients, who had made many spirits or creatures to help them. But these ones had turned against them, twisting their purposes to evil, becoming a danger that had to be locked away.

Uki remembered finding the shattered pink,

diamond-like crystal that had held them, as he staggered through the Icebark Forest almost mad with grief for his mother who had just died. If it hadn't been for Iffrit driving him on, he might never have started on this quest. The fiery little being had been desperate, afraid. But determined that Uki would take on the task.

Gaunch, the first spirit he had captured, had tried to starve and famish the world around him. Valkus, the second one, had wanted to spread war and battle everywhere. But Charice ... she had been more subtle, more terrible.

Her mission was disease. She sought to fill every living thing with it. To corrupt and change everything around her until she and her servants ruled it all. And she had begun already.

Uki could feel it. A plague spreading out like a flowing blot of ink, seeping from the heart of the marshes – poisoning, twisting, infecting ...

He broke his mind free before he could see any more and fell to his knees, gasping for breath. He half expected to see the grass dying around him, the bees and butterflies that flitted around the yellow gorse flowers dropping to the ground, writhing and dying.

'What is it, Uki?' Kree jumped down from Mooka, her long-eared, kangaroo-legged jerboa, and rushed to his side. 'Did you see it? Is it bad?'

'It's ... horrible,' Uki whispered. 'She's called Charice and she brings plague and disease. She wants to infect every living thing in the world.'

'And she's in those marshes?' Kree asked.

'Yes,' said Uki. 'Right in the heart of the fen. And she's already started. We don't have much time to stop her.'

Jori kicked at a clump of heather. 'The heart of the fen. That's just typical. There's a whole load of nice, dry, civilised warrens on the other side. What's wrong with trying to take over the world from one of those?'

'We could try stopping off at one of the warrens ahead?' Kree suggested. 'They must have inns to stay in. We could have a good night's sleep or two before we have to wade through all that swamp.'

Jori nodded at that, the thought of a feather bed and a decent meal cheering her up a little.

Uki still stared out at the marshes that, just a few moments ago, had seemed full of life and promise. Now he couldn't help imagining them poisoned and ruined, the source of a plague that was hungry to eat the whole world.

Leaving the hilltop, they began to wind their way down the spidery track that led to Mudstock warren in the valley below. It was close enough to reach by dusk and hopefully had a decent inn.

Honeybees buzzed about them as they walked and red kites circled lazily overhead. It was a pleasant summer evening and, despite the shadow of the horrors Uki had sensed in his vision, he was beginning to relax and enjoy himself. Until Jori spoke, that is.

'There's something else,' she said, as they clambered over a wooden stile set into a tumbledown drystone wall. 'Something I should warn you about.'

'*Mik jibbadan lashki*,' said Kree. 'You mean besides the plague spirit in the fen, the Endwatch who are chasing us *and* your evil cousin?'

'Go on,' said Uki, as Jori rolled her eyes. He could see that she was tense again. Her ears were flat against her head, and her brow was knitted together in one of her stern frowns. She looked almost as edgy as she had when they passed the Coldwood.

'There's a clan that lives on the far side of the marshes. A shadow clan – assassins, like Clan Septys . . . except a lot worse. We're likely to come across them, if not in Mudstock, then in the warrens beyond.'

'Worse than your family of poisoning murderers?' Kree had helped Mooka hop over the stile and was now hoisting herself into his saddle again. 'How could anyone be scarier than that?'

'Easily,' said Jori. 'They can be from Clan Shrike.'

'What's so bad about them?' Uki asked.

'They're meaner than a pack of starved weasels,' said Jori. 'They hire themselves out as killers, like my clan, but they like to do things close up. They use the blades they have on the forearms of their crimson armour. And there are rumours that they take their victims' bodies back to their warren and put them on spikes. Some say they even do it *before* they're actually dead. Their place is called Bloodthorn. I've never seen it, but I've heard terrible stories.'

'Why will they be at this Mud-plop warren?'

Kree had begun to look around, her paw resting on the half spear she'd found during their battle in the twin cities. It now jutted from her bedroll, ready to be used on any enemy that got in her way.

'Mud*stock*,' Jori said. 'Because, as well as sticking pointy things in rabbits, they work for the Emperor. They're in charge of collecting taxes and getting rid of smugglers.'

'What are "smugglers"?' Uki asked. 'Some kind of creature?'

Jori laughed. 'No. Smugglers are rabbits. They take things that are brought into Hulstland from other realms, and they sell them.'

'That doesn't sound so bad,' said Kree. 'Why do these Spike-rabbits want to stop them?'

'*Shrike*,' said Jori. 'Although "spike" might be better. The problem is the Emperor says that everything that comes from other countries: food, cloth, wine ... has to arrive in one of his ports, and the rabbits buying it have to give him some of the money they will make from it. It's called "tax" or "duty". It's one of the things that makes him so rich.

'Anyway, some rabbits don't want to pay tax, so

they arrange for the stuff to be dropped off by boat at secret beaches and coves near the edge of the fen. Then they sneak it through the swamps and sell it to the warrens on the far side. They make good money, other rabbits get the goods cheaper, *but* the Emperor loses out on his share.'

'Ah.' Kree nodded her head. 'So it's a kind of stealing? And the Emperor has laws against it? Like if you steal a jerboa and the chieftain has you staked out on the plain for the buzzards.'

'Yes,' said Jori. 'Except Clan Shrike will be the ones catching you, and it will be much more painful than getting eaten alive by a buzzard. They hate my clan too. Septys and Shrike have been at war with each other for centuries.'

'Shouldn't you take off your brooch, then?' Uki said, pointing at the coiled silver serpent on Jori's shoulder.

'Kether above!' Jori snatched it off in a blink and shoved it in her pack. 'Good thinking, Uki.'

'And just in time,' said Kree. 'Here is Mud-plop warren. I hope they have a lovely inn with a good stable for Mooka.'

'It's Mud*st*—' Jori began, but Kree was already trotting ahead, into the settlement. Keeping an eye out for rabbits in scary armour, Jori and Uki followed.

*

'What do you mean, there's no inn?' Jori, usually calm and confident when speaking to people, raised her voice loud enough to make Uki cringe. Her dreams of a soft bed and a belly full of supper had just vanished, leaving behind the beginnings of a temper tantrum.

'Just what I says.' They were talking to an old she-rabbit, who was wearing a patched, hooded cloak and carrying a basket of lettuces. 'We don't have no inns here. The priest doesn't like it. Strangers can find a bed at the church, though. A stable too, for your . . . hoppy rat-thing.'

The old rabbit shuffled off, leaving Jori shaking her head and Kree fuming. Uki took a moment to look around the warren.

They had just come through some wide wooden gates, and they could see another pair in the distance, opposite. Surrounding them was a stone wall, as high as two rabbits, with a walkway at the top on which a few guards stood watch.

Inside the wall were lots of grass-covered mounds, each with two or three chimneys poking out. They all had a wood or stone front, with a door and a window. As Jori had said, they looked like a mixture of house and burrow, and seemed to be very cosy.

Most were homes for the Mudstock rabbits, but one or two had carved wooden signs outside. Uki spotted a grocery, a pie shop and a blacksmith's. At the centre of the warren was a strange-looking building. Made of stone, with a turf roof, it had a squat tower at one end, the top of which was covered in numbers made out of polished bronze. As the sun began to set, the bronze sparkled and glinted as if it was burning with golden light.

'I guess that's the church,' he said. 'We should probably see if they have a place for us to stay before dark.'

Jori nodded, still sulking about the lack of inns, and they wandered over with Kree cursing behind them.

'*Hoppy rat-thing* . . . hasn't she ever seen a jerboa? *Pok ha boc!*'

Before they knocked on the door, Jori stopped them.

'I'm guessing you don't know too much about churches of Kether, Uki?'

Uki shook his head. There was only one god in the Ice Wastes – Zeryth, the brutal lord of snow. His mother had taught him about the twin goddesses, Estra and Nixha, but he hadn't yet learned much about Kether, Hulstland's god of order and number.

'Don't worry.' Jori patted him on the shoulder. 'You don't need to know much. Just don't mention any other religions in front of the priest. And avoid saying the numbers four and fourteen. Or any two numbers that add up to them.'

'And don't do anything fourteen times,' added Kree. 'Especially not flicking your ears. Or touching your nose. They hate that.'

'What about all the other numbers?' Uki asked. Being told *not* to do something always made him want to do it, and his ears had already started jumping about on their own.

'Three is good,' said Jori. 'Do everything three times, if you can. Seven also. And nine and twelve are OK.'

'Eight?' Uki's head was beginning to spin.

'If it's a feast day,' said Jori. 'And ten is good on a full moon.'

They were still throwing numbers at Uki when the church doors opened and a robed rabbit stepped out. He was dressed in layers of thick purple material embroidered all over with gold thread. On his head was a tall, funny-shaped hat, also purple, and he clutched a staff that was topped off with a carved spiral. He smiled kindly at them, although his dark eyes were serious beneath a frowning brow.

'Ninefold blessings on you,' he said, touching three fingers to his forehead. 'My name is Father Klepper. How may Kether help you on this fine evening?'

'We're ... um ... looking for a place to stay the night,' said Uki. He tried bobbing his head nine times, but lost count and added a couple of extra ones for good measure. Then he had a panic, in case he'd done fourteen by mistake, and added a few more.

'Is there something wrong with you?' asked Father Klepper.

'Forgive my friend,' said Jori, trying not to laugh. 'He is very tired. We've travelled all the way from the twin cities, you see.'

'All that way, on your own?' The priest looked shocked. 'Then you must come in and take shelter. Poor, poor children. And there's a stable behind the church for your ... gangly weasel.'

'HE'S A ...' Kree began to shout, but Uki and Jori quickly bundled themselves inside the church and shut the door behind them, hoping that the thick wood would muffle most of their friend's yelling.

They found themselves in a long room with a high roof. A window of tinted glass at the far end was letting in the rosy light of the setting sun. It seemed to glow, and filled the church with overlapping patches of colour. Uki stared at it, hypnotised. He raised his hands and smiled at the streaks of painted light tinting his fur.

'Beautiful, isn't it?' said Father Klepper. 'We are just about to perform the evening count, if you would like to join us. After that, we will have some supper.'

39

He led them past rows of benches, where several other rabbits sat in prayer. Most looked like ordinary villagers, with simple cloaks and homespun clothes. One or two wore purple robes, like the Father.

'What's the evening count?' Uki whispered to Jori, as quietly as he could. But the sound still managed to echo around the silent church and made him wince.

'They count Kether's sacred numbers every morning and night,' Jori whispered back 'Just open and close your mouth and pretend you know them.'

They sat down at the end of one of the benches and watched as Father Klepper walked to the front of the church, where there was an enormous mural of a rabbit with four outstretched arms. Lines ran between his limbs and ears, and there were numbers squiggled everywhere. It all looked very mysterious and solemn.

'Ninefold blessings,' Father Klepper began. 'Please join me in counting the sacred numbers of the universe, as told to us by Our Lord. Let us begin. One, one, two, three, five, eight, thirteen, twenty-one, thirty-four, fifty-five, eighty-nine . . .'

Soon, all the rabbits were joining in, their voices echoing around the church. Uki opened and closed his mouth in time, watching Jori from the corner of his eye and hoping that he wouldn't be spotted. **What if they ask you what the next number is?** His dark voice had been quiet since the battle with Valkus, but now it decided to chip in, just to make him feel worse.

Luckily, it was soon over. As the rest of the rabbits began to file out of the church, back to their burrow-houses, Father Klepper motioned for Uki and Jori to follow him. They went through a small side door, which led to a courtyard. Kree was in one of the stalls, rubbing down Mooka's fur with a handful of hay. A tired-looking piebald rat stood beside them, chewing a mouthful of oats.

'We shall have supper in my house,' said Father Klepper, 'and then you may all sleep in the stable.'

It was a far cry from the feather beds and fireplaces they had been hoping for, but it was better than sleeping on the ground again, Uki supposed. Trying not to look too disappointed, they all followed the priest into his burrow.

Because the house-burrows were dug down into the ground, they appeared to be bigger on the inside than the outside. It took a little while for Uki to get used to the sensation, and Kree was even more confused.

But the place was very cosy. There was a large fireplace, a dining table in the middle and shelves covering the walls, all stuffed with books and scrolls. Uki wondered if they would be filled with numbers.

'Please,' said Father Klepper. 'Be seated.'

As they pulled chairs around the table, the Father went into a small pantry at the back and began to bring out bowls of food and plates. He laid them on the table, adding cups and a jug of water. Soon, there was a tasty dinner spread before them: dandelion leaves, crusty bread, pickled beetroots, dried parsnips and carrots.

'So,' said Father Klepper, as they began to load their plates, 'what leads three children to be wandering the Realms without a parent or guardian to take care of them?'

Uki's mind instantly went blank. He froze, mid-mouthful, and stared at the Father, trying to think of some kind of explanation. Fortunately, Jori was good at this sort of thing. She spoke up quickly, while Kree was chewing and unable to ruin it.

'We're on our way to stay with our uncle,' she said. 'Our mother is too ill to come with us, and our father sadly passed away, Kether bless him. We're travelling to Herongate warren, but thought it would be lovely to see some of the famous fens on the way.'

'Ah, the Fenlands,' said Father Klepper, shaking his head. 'You had best stay away from them. A numberless hole of chaos and crime. I have tried several times to bring them the digits of Our Lord, but have been turned away. Sometimes with violence.'

'We were just planning a brief visit,' Jori continued. 'There are said to be many rare and beautiful bird species there. And the customs of the rabbits are supposed to be fascinating. Do they really dress in frogskin?'

'They are savages,' said the priest, his ears beginning to tremble. 'Just the thought of them and their beastly ways makes me shiver ...'

'But can't you tell us anything about them?

Perhaps, if they weren't such a mystery, we wouldn't be so curious to see them.'

'I can tell you very little,' said Father Klepper. 'But if it keeps you out of that godless place ... Reedwic warren is the most civilised part of it. You should be safe there. Beyond that ... the tribes that live in the Fenlands themselves are best avoided.'

'Are there many?' Uki asked. 'Tribes, I mean ...'

'There are two that I know of,' said Father Klepper. 'Two large clans or families. The Maggitches and the Gurdles. They are at war with each other, and have been for generations. It's a bitter feud. I'm surprised they haven't wiped each other out by now.'

'Sounds like the plains tribes,' said Kree, around a mouthful of carrot. 'They quarrel for months then have a big party to make up.'

'There's no "making up" with these families,' said Father Klepper. 'They're too primitive for that. They worship strange old swamp gods and paddle around that maze of water and mud in boats and rafts. They make their living – when they're not trying to kill each other – by smuggling goods across the swamp. They would steal the very cloak from your back as soon as look at you. No, that place is forsaken by Kether, and rightly so. If you have any sense, you'll head back towards the Coldwood and follow the road around the fen. It will take longer, but you'll arrive in one piece.'

Uki had questions about the changes he had sensed in the swamp, but Father Klepper seemed too upset by mention of the fen tribes to answer anything else. They ate the rest of the meal in silence and then made their way out to the stable.

'Think on what I have told you,' said Father Klepper, as he left them for the night. 'Keep away from the swamp. Stick to the parts of the world that have been ordered and numbered.'

'Well,' said Kree, when the Father had gone back to his house. 'He was a cheery one, wasn't he? All that counting and praying has made him dull as ditchwater.'

'He had a point, though,' said Jori, as she spread out her cloak on a pile of straw. 'The Fenlands are going to be very dangerous. We should try to find a guide of some kind at Reedwic.'

'Poor Mooka,' said Kree. 'He's going to hate all

that water and gloopy mud. Swamps are for voles and otters, not jerboas.'

Uki curled himself in his cloak at the doorway of the stable, so he could look up and see the stars. The more he heard about the fen, the more worried he became. Shrikes, warring tribes, a gathering plague . . . how was he supposed to deal with all that? If it wasn't for Jori and Kree, he would be completely helpless, but at the same time he couldn't shake the feeling that he was leading them into danger. Again.

The stars moved slowly across the sky as his worries turned themselves over and over in his head. At some point, his eyes drifted shut and he slept . . .

*

The dream started almost immediately.

Except it wasn't a dream. He was with Necripha again, seeing through her eyes, hearing her thoughts. There was a link between Necripha and Iffrit. Sometimes, usually when he slept, he got a glimpse into her mind. It was never very pleasant.

This time, the witch was standing in a copse of trees, deep in shadow. Uki could hear a river running nearby and there was a stretch of open, grassy land in front, with a thick pine forest in the distance. It looked like the Coldwood.

A road ran past the copse, wider than the one they had followed. It had deep cart ruts and lots of potholes. It led towards another walled settlement, off to the west. Bleakridge, Uki guessed. Jori had said it was the only warren north of the woods. Quiet and sleeping now, its gates were shut for the night. White chimney smoke from the slumbering burrows stood out against the black sky like chalk scribbles on a slate.

Uki could sense that Necripha was waiting for something. He could feel the waves of tension and impatience flowing through her. Her ears twitched, her fingers tapped. She was angry too. Probably because Uki had slipped away from her in Syn. That, or the fact he had captured Valkus before she could lure him over to her side.

A movement on the road drew her vision. She could see some figures coming her way, sneaking out of Bleakridge. One was vast and bulky (*probably Balto, her henchman*, Uki thought), the others smaller, hooded rabbits.

As they drew closer, Necripha stepped from the trees, making the smaller figures bow and grovel.

'Mistress, mistress!' Uki heard them whining.

'Enough!' Necripha hissed. 'What has taken you worm-brained idiots so long? Didn't I tell you we were short of time?'

'Sorry, mistress,' said Balto. He shoved one of the hooded followers forwards. 'We had to wait for this one to arrive from Axen.'

Necripha glared at the rabbit until it started to cry. 'Beat him!' she commanded. Uki felt the old witch glow with pleasure as Balto thumped the cowering creature to the ground. When he was finished, she took another look at her recruits. 'Five rabbits. Is this all we could manage?'

'The others were too far away to get here in time,' said Balto. 'More have heard the call. They will be meeting us in Herongate.'

'We're not going to Herongate!' Necripha hit her servant with the end of her staff. The stick simply bounced off his mountainous shoulders, without even making him flinch. 'I can sense the spirit and that interfering little rabbit. They're behind the Coldwood, in the swamps. *That* is where we need to go.'

Uki saw one or two of the new Endwatch servants shudder at the mention of the Fenlands, but Necripha didn't notice, or care. She was already on the march, heading east towards the sea. If she walked all night, she would soon be on the path that Uki and his friends had followed, and after that it was just a day's journey to Mudstock.

'Can you hear me, spying little brat?' Necripha tapped the bandage on her head. Uki shivered and squirmed in his sleep, remembering that terrible third eye that was hidden beneath it. 'Are you in my head? You and that cursed guardian spirit of yours?'

Go away, Uki willed his dream-self to shout, wishing the words could flow through the night and blast Necripha off her feet. *Leave us alone, you evil old hag. Isn't our job hard enough without you chasing us?*

'I know where you are,' Necripha continued, unable to hear any of Uki's curses. 'I'm coming to get you, child. I have servants looking for you, everywhere you go. And this time you won't escape, no matter how many clever friends you have to help you.'

With a jolt, Uki woke up. He had kicked off his cloak during his vision, and rolled from his pile of straw. Now he was shivering – more from fright than the cold.

Kree, Jori and Mooka all slept soundly nearby. Snoring and twitching, completely unaware of the evil just the other side of the woods. How Uki wished he could be so innocent.

Still trembling, he curled back up in his cloak as best he could. Not to sleep, though. No. The thought of what he might see in his dreams was too terrifying.

Fighting to keep his eyes open, he stared up at the sky and waited until morning.

CHAPTER THREE

Needle

I t was an hour or so after dawn when the others awoke. Father Klepper brought them each a bowl of hot porridge and honey, and they sat and ate while watching the Mudstock rabbits emerge from their burrows and go about their day.

Uki's thoughts were still on his vision from the night before. He considered mentioning it to the others, but decided it was best not to. Jori was already worried about Clan Shrike, and Kree kept fretting over Mooka being in wet marshland. He didn't like to give them yet more bad news.

51

Even so, he wanted to be on the move right away. The more distance they put between themselves and Necripha, the better.

'You're eating that very quickly,' said Jori. 'In a hurry to get somewhere?'

Uki cringed. He really wasn't very good at keeping things secret. 'No ... well, yes. I just want to get into the fen. We need to stop Charice before her plague starts to spread.' He reached up to tap one of the empty crystals on his remaining spear tips. The place the evil spirit would hopefully soon be calling home.

'Hmm. You look tired.' Jori was staring at him with her steely grey eyes. It was a very difficult gaze to hide from.

'Oh, I just slept badly,' said Uki. Which wasn't *completely* a lie. 'Tickly straw ... bit cold. You know ...'

Seeming convinced, Jori went back to her porridge. Then as soon as they were all finished, they dropped the bowls back to Father Klepper and went on their way, with a final warning about the godless, cursed marshes as a parting gift.

Reedwic was two hours' walk away, along a straight and well-kept track. The land on either side was packed with fields, each one bursting with sprouting, swelling crops. Rabbits moved between the rows of growing vegetables, watering, weeding and hoeing. Uki could smell cabbages, turnips and carrots, tomatoes, potatoes and radishes. The air was thick with a planty, earthy scent that made his mouth water.

'They call the land between the Coldwood and the Fenlands the "salad bowl",' Jori explained. 'It's especially damp and fertile. Good soil. Although it has been known to flood in winter.'

Uki spotted farmers' houses in amongst the patches of vegetables. Some were made of wood and raised up on stilts. *What a sweet, simple life*, he thought. *Tending and growing your crops in the sunshine. Nothing to worry about except caterpillars and the weather.* **And the plague that's coming,** his dark voice added. **This place will be the first to die, if you don't capture Charice.**

At the thought of the spirit's name, Uki could sense her. A growing, pulsing sickness, now closer than ever before. He stopped his daydreaming and quickened his pace.

It wasn't long before Reedwic came into view. They could see the stone wall with its gate and guard towers. Red and green banners flew from flagpoles, and a stream of carts laden with crops were heading in and out. It might have seemed a bustling, merry place, if Kree hadn't spotted the guards on either side of the entrance.

'Look,' she said, pointing. 'Aren't those soldiers wearing armour? Crimson armour?'

They all knew what that meant. Uki peered towards them, but his eyes weren't as sharp as the little plains rabbit's. It wasn't until they were much closer that he saw the blood-red plates of the guards' uniforms. Closer still and he could see three metal spikes jutting from the vambraces on each of their forearms. He shuddered, imagining how the Shrikes might use them to finish off their enemies. 'I'm sure they'll let us through,' he said, more to cheer himself up than anything. Jori and Kree just looked at him, worried.

There was a short queue of carts at the gate,

which they joined. Trying with all his might to look harmless and innocent, Uki snatched glimpses of the Shrike guards as they edged closer to the gate.

One wore a helmet with a face mask like a beak. The other had short grey fur and had daubed a stripe of black warpaint across his eyes. He wasn't sure which one looked the scariest. They were examining each cart, poking and prodding the contents with their spears, before letting them into the warren.

The line of rabbits moved all too quickly, and soon they were standing in the gateway, facing the Shrikes. The spikes on their arms glinted like the fangs of an adder, basking in the sun. They were bronze, Uki saw, and honed to points so sharp it hurt even to look at them. It was all he could do not to tremble. He stepped up to face them, held his breath and . . .

'Attention!'

A voice shouted out from inside the gate. Instantly, the guards snapped themselves as upright and straight as freshly placed fence poles. Another two Shrikes marched out of the warren, and Uki could hear Jori give a quiet groan beside him.

'Prepare for inspection by Captain Needle!' the taller, broader Shrike bellowed.

The Captain stepped up to each guard in turn, checking over their armour and testing the points of their arm spikes with a finger. Satisfied, she nodded, then reached up to remove her beaked helmet. Underneath was a fierce rabbit, grey-furred, with the same streak of black paint across her eyes as the guard.

'Back to your posts,' she said, then turned to look at Uki and his friends. Her gaze was dark, cold and predatory. Empty of all feeling and emotion except, perhaps, cruelty.

'What have we here?' She walked across to where Uki and his friends stood. 'Three little strangers, all on their own? A plains rabbit, and two with some very interesting armour and weapons. Are those spears? With crystal heads? How unusual.'

Uki waited for Jori to do the talking, as she usually did, but this time she was strangely silent. From the corner of his eye, Uki saw she had pulled her cloak across her body, hiding the silver-topped flask of dusk potion on her belt. Next to her, Kree was clearing her throat to speak. Knowing she would probably say something tactless enough to get them all killed, Uki realised it was up to him.

'We're on our way to our aunt . . . I mean, uncle!' he blurted.

'Really?' said Needle, leaning closer to peer at the red and yellow gems in his spear harness. 'An aunt-uncle? Here in Reedwic?'

'No, in Herongate.' Uki tried to remember the story that Jori had spun to Father Klepper. It had sounded so natural and convincing when she said it. 'We wanted to travel through the fen. It has many rare and beautiful species of frogskinned rabbits. And the customs of the birds are fascinating.'

'Are they indeed?' Needle smiled, showing white teeth that seemed far too sharp for a rabbit. 'You must tell me about it during your stay.'

'M-must I?'

'Oh yes.' Needle's gaze moved on to Jori, sliding over her fine leather armour before resting on her belt. For a dreadful moment, Uki thought she was going to snatch the cloak away and spot her flask. 'I spend most of my time wandering around the town, keeping an eye on things. I'm sure we'll bump into each other again.'

'That would be ... nice,' said Uki, sounding entirely unconvincing.

'And while you are here ... if anyone offers to sell you any wine or cloth, you will let me know, won't you? We have a terrible problem with smugglers, you see.'

'Of course,' said Uki. He nodded and tried to smile, although it came out as more of a grimace. 'We'll let you know right away.'

'Enjoy your visit.' Needle grinned again, then she stepped aside and ushered them into Reedwic with a sweeping gesture that, from any other rabbit, would have been welcoming.

The three friends scurried past. Looking over his shoulder, Uki saw Needle's blank stare following them, until finally they were lost amongst the crowd of carts and bustling rabbits.

'*Nam ukku ulla*,' said Kree. 'She was a mean one!'

Jori put a paw on Uki's arm. 'Sorry,' she said. 'I dared not speak. I was certain she was going to recognise me as Septys.'

'Don't worry,' said Uki. 'At least they let us in. I thought for a minute they were going to arrest us on the doorstep.'

Jori looked back towards the gateway, a stark frown on her face. 'I believe she only let us in so she would be able to keep an eye on us. The quicker we can leave this place, the better.'

'Why are you two so worried?' Kree reached down from Mooka's back to ruffle their ears. 'Uki is strong enough to throw all those spiky rabbits from here to Icebark Forest, and Jori could slice them into salad before they finished a blink. And if it came to the worst, we could all jump on Mooka and race home to the plains. We are the Outcasts – the meanest rabbits in all Hulstland. It is *them* who should be frightened of *us*.'

Uki laughed, even though he didn't share his friend's confidence. Keeping a wary eye out for Captain Needle, they began to search Reedwic for a guide.

*

Even though they were almost neighbours, Reedwic looked a very different place to Mudstock. Almost all the houses were made of wood and raised on stilts. Steps led up to the front doors, and they seemed to be the place everyone sat, enjoying the sunshine. There were rabbits outside every building, chatting to neighbours, drinking tea or playing musical instruments. A kind of long-necked, round-bodied lute seemed to be the most popular. It had a twangy sound that made Uki want to tap his feet and dance.

The stone wall surrounding everything was only a semicircle. At the far end of town was a wide, fast-running river, and on the other side of that, the Fenlands.

There were docks beside the river, and many boats and barges loading and unloading. Uki spotted several different styles of craft, and sails of many patterns and colours.

Also, unlike Mudstock, there were more than a few inns and taverns. Good places to look for a guide and maybe some information about what was happening in the marshes.

'This one here has a stable,' Kree called. She was pointing up at a painted sign that showed a tall scrawny bird with a frog clutched in its long beak.

'The Greedy Heron,' said Jori, reading the runes beneath the picture.

'Do you think it will be safe?' Uki asked. Something about the meeting with Captain Needle had set him on edge. Or perhaps it was the lingering tendrils of his dream about Necripha. Maybe even the constant pulsing at the back of his mind that came from Charice, hidden somewhere in the marshes.

'I'm sure we'll be fine,' said Jori. 'Although ... I have a feeling we're being watched.'

'Me too,' said Uki. He looked around the crowds of rabbits in the street, but couldn't spot anything out of the ordinary. 'Maybe we're just worrying about the Shrikes?'

'Maybe,' said Jori. She followed Kree into the courtyard of the Greedy Heron, and Uki was about to join her when he noticed a movement on one of the wooden stilts of the inn. Stepping closer, he could see it was an insect of some kind. A fat one. It seemed to be struggling – perhaps caught in a spider's web?

Closer still and he could see it was some kind of fly. But it wasn't trapped by anything. Instead, it was trying to move on stunted, misshapen legs. Its body was bloated, bulging out in strange places and oozing thick yellow pus. It looked like it had too many eyes and its wings were lopsided. They buzzed and flapped in vain, trying to lift its bulk into the air.

Charice, Uki thought. This was one of her diseased creatures. They had already started to spread, out of the heart of the fen and into places where rabbits lived. That thing could be filled with plague, sent here to pass it on to any rabbit that touched it.

Carefully, Uki drew one of the spears from his harness and used the butt to crush the fly. It went *pop*, releasing a trickle of foul liquid, which made Uki feel more than a little queasy. He wiped his spear on a patch of weeds several times, until he was sure it was clean, then trotted after his friends, wondering how many more poisoned insects were in the air, crawling through the buildings . . .

*

Once Mooka had been safely stabled, they climbed the steps to the inn itself. There were quite a few rabbits inside, eating their lunch or passing the time while their ships were loaded. Uki spotted several lops, with their enormous, droopy ears, a few angoras, with masses of tufty fur, spotted harlequins, tiny dwarf rabbits and even a towering giant rabbit, who took up a whole corner by the fire.

But most of the customers had short ears, long legs and large feet with splayed toes. These seemed to be the inhabitants of the Fenlands, and they all spoke with a deep, rich accent, full of 'oohs' and 'arrs'.

After a quick scan to make sure there weren't any Shrikes about, the three of them found a table near the window. Uki peered up at the sky, looking for clouds of black flies, swarming from the marshes.

'What are you staring at?' Jori asked. 'Started birdwatching already?'

'Oh, nothing,' said Uki. 'Just ... checking for flies.'

'Flies?' Jori was about to ask more, when a bar rabbit came over. One of the fen locals, he spoke with a thick, buzzing accent.

'Art'noon,' he said. 'Just the three of you for nammet?'

'Nammet?' Kree frowned. 'What kind of word is that?'

'It means food,' said the bar rabbit. 'Bain't you from round here?'

'Do I *look* like I'm from round here?' Kree pointed to the red-painted stripes on her ears and cheeks.

'Hmm,' said the bar rabbit, beginning to sound annoyed. 'Well, we has marsh orchid salad, sweetgrass gumbo, eel pie and stickleback surprise.'

'What's the surprise?' Uki asked.

'You finds out when you eats it,' said the rabbit.

'*Pok ha boc*,' said Kree. 'I don't like the sound of swamp food.'

'These be *fens*, not *swamps*.'

'Mud, water and gloop,' said Kree. 'That makes a *swamp*, whatever you want to call it.'

'Perhaps you should let me order, Kree,' said Jori. She gave the little rabbit a glare as sharp as the edge on her sky-metal sword. 'The sweetgrass gumbo sounds nice, don't you think, Uki?'

Uki nodded. He was only half listening. Being around so many rabbits was still very new to him, even after his adventures in the twin cities. For most of his life, it had been just him and his mother in their little hut. Now there was so much to *see* all the time. His eyes were drawn to something new every second.

He had just seen a fen rabbit in a purple cloak slip out of the inn, glancing back at them several times as he left. Was that something to worry about? Or just a local rabbit staring at the outsiders? How did you know who could be trusted – whether they were kind and friendly or wished you harm? The outside world was too confusing.

I miss Mother so much. A picture of their hut appeared in his mind, heartbreak clear. His mother putting a fresh batch of dried pots into her kiln, him building a castle of stones next to her. Everything was so safe and simple then.

'Uki?' Jori's paw on his arm brought him back to the present. He wiped a tear from his eye and looked about. It seemed Kree had just said something else offensive, and the waiter was looking even grumpier. And to make things worse, some of the local rabbits had begun to notice.

'Do there be a problem?' A big fen rabbit stepped

over to their table. His ears were tight back against his boulder-shaped head and his eyes were narrowed in a frown. Two more came to join him. Uki noticed how the fur on their wide feet was matted and spiky with dried mud. Their clothes were spattered with it too, and at their belts hung long bronze skinning knives. Well used, but sharp. These were hunters of some kind. Proud and local and dangerous.

'No, no,' said Jori. 'We were just ordering some food.' She gave the rabbits a broad, friendly smile, but at the same time her paw had gone to the flask at her belt. Uki tensed, ready to get in between these scary swamp rabbits and Kree if they tried to touch her.

'Sounds like you be having a problem with our fen,' said the big rabbit. He ignored Jori and glared at Kree. 'Sounds like I might have to put you across my knee and give you a good spanking.'

The other swamp rabbits laughed at this and Kree stood up on her chair, bringing her face closer to the ringleader.

'I'm not a *child*, you know. I'm ten years old!' She put her hands on her hips and glared.

'That's old enough for a whooping, wouldn't you

say, boys?' The big rabbit's friends laughed some more. 'We don't take kindly to folk coming here and insulting our home.'

'This has all been a misunderstanding,' said Jori. 'Perhaps we could buy you a drink to apologise?'

That isn't going to work, Uki thought. These rabbits were bullies and they had sniffed out someone weaker than them. Bullies never gave up when they had easy prey, he knew that all too well.

Except Uki and Jori weren't as vulnerable as they looked. They could make short work of the Reedwic rabbits if they wanted. But that would draw attention to them, which would make it impossible to find a guide and slip into the fen unnoticed. And that was what their whole mission depended on.

Uki looked around the inn, seeing if there was a quick way out. All the other customers were staring now, and through the window, in the street beyond, he could see a patrol of three Shrikes coming this way. If they did try to defend themselves, they would be spotted.

'Jori,' he said through gritted teeth, grabbing her arm. 'Jori, look *outside*.'

'What do you think, boys?' The big rabbit had begun to roll up his sleeves. 'Three little brats and three of us. How about we take one each and show them what happens to naughty kittens when they talk slop about us?'

Pop. Jori's thumb flicked the cap off her flask. Kree clenched her little fists and held them up in front of her face.

This is it, thought Uki. *We're going to end up spiked by Shrikes or thrown in prison before our quest even gets started.*

CHAPTER FOUR

The Stranger

'Now just hold on a minute, boys.'

A gruff voice came from the bar, followed by the sound of someone walking across the floorboards. *Clump-clonk, clump-clonk.*

Uki took his eyes from the trio of angry locals to see a strange figure coming towards them.

A rabbit? Could it be?

The newcomer was so scarred and mauled it was difficult to tell *what* he was. He leaned on a crutch, his left leg having been replaced with a wooden peg. The skin of his face and arms was scorched of almost every single hair. It was puckered, pink and torn – seared all over. His ears were tattered stubs and his left eye covered by a patch.

But the thing that really made Uki gape – and that silenced the Reedwic bullies too – was his right arm. Or rather, what had taken its place.

It was missing from the elbow down, and fitted on the stump was a heavy blacksmith's hammer. The shaft was polished walnut, wrapped in leather. The head, a thundering piece of sky metal that could crack a rabbit's skull as if it were a robin's egg. He lifted it up and rested it on the table in front of Kree.

Clump.

There was a moment of silence as the three bullies stared at the scarred rabbit. He stared back, his good eye unblinking. The melted skin around his mouth slowly pulled back in a smile. A smile that he might give a piece of hot steel, just before he pounded it flat.

'Ch … Charcoal,' the big rabbit said. 'We was just having a chat with these 'ere nippers. A spot of fun, like.'

'Well,' said Charcoal. 'It appears the fun's over now. Unless you want to have some with me?'

'No!' The big rabbit almost jumped out of his muddy rags. 'I mean, no thank you. We'll just be going about our business now. Won't we, lads?'

'You do that,' said Charcoal. He left his hammer resting on the table as the three bullies scuttled away. When they were gone, he turned to the waiter, who had been edging back to the bar. 'You can fetch these young rabbits their gumbo now,' he said. 'And perhaps with some complimentary drinks thrown in.'

The waiter bobbed his head like a priest of Kether gone crazy and dashed back out to the kitchen.

'Thank you,' said Jori. 'But we didn't need your help.'

'No,' said Kree. 'We were about to kick those frog-lickers back into their mudholes!'

Charcoal laughed, a deep, husky sound, as if his lungs had been baked as thoroughly as the rest of him. 'I'm sure you were,' he said. 'But I thought I might lend a paw. Even though I only have one to spare.'

'Would you like to join us?' Uki asked. He had noticed the Shrike patrol pass by without so much as a blink at the inn. The scarred stranger had saved them, without even realising it, and Uki felt a rush of gratitude. Kree and Jori had no idea how close they'd come to serious trouble.

'Why, that's very kind of you,' said Charcoal. 'But I wouldn't like to intrude.'

'I insist,' said Uki. Jori looked at him with an eyebrow raised. Uki waggled his at her. *This rabbit might be a good guide*, he was trying to say, although he didn't think she understood.

'Then I shall accept.' Charcoal pulled over a chair, rested his crutch against the back of it and sat down. As the young rabbits watched, he grasped the shaft of his hammer and twisted it. There was a *click* and it came away from the metal cuff on his arm. He set it down on the floor with a *thunk* that shook the table.

'Everyone round here calls me Charcoal, by the way,' he said. 'Because I look like I was left in the fire too long. But friends shorten it to "Coal".'

'What ... what *happened* to you?' Kree was staring at his furless skin, mouth open. 'You look like a fire demon chewed you up and spat you out.

72

Or like an ogre roasted you on a spit, then ate your arm and leg and didn't like the taste.'

'*Kree!*' Jori slapped her hand on the table. 'Didn't anyone ever tell you that you don't *have* to say every single thought that comes into your head?'

Coal waved his hand and gave that smoky laugh again. 'It's all right. Don't worry. I've heard just about every mean thing that could be said about me. I know I don't exactly look pretty, but there's nothing I can do about it.'

'Have you always been ... different?' Uki knew all about being treated badly because of how you looked. He had spent most of his life hidden away from his tribe, thanks to his split-colour fur and mismatched eyes. He had felt the sadness, the unfairness, of folk calling him evil and wicked before they'd even taken the time to speak two words to him.

'No, not always.' Coal gave a sad smile. 'I was a miner once. Chief Engineer. I worked in Eisenfell, digging out sky metal from the crater around the city. I was paid good money. I had a house, a wife ... and then one day we were digging a new shaft. We came across a pocket of gas. One of the lads had an uncovered candle and . . . *boom.*

'I was the only one that survived. But I couldn't work in the mine again. In fact, I couldn't work anywhere for a long while. I lost my house . . . everything.

'Then I left the city and started to wander. I had worked as a blacksmith when I was younger, so I started doing odd metalwork jobs here and there. And I grew to love life on the road – go where you will, nobody being your boss – so I became a travelling smith.'

'Have you been in the Fenlands long?' Uki asked.

'A good few months,' said Coal. 'I've just come back from deep in the marshes. Did some work for the Gurdles.'

'One of the feuding tribes?' Uki said, remembering what Father Klepper had told them.

'Yes. I've worked for them a fair bit now. Enough to be under their protection. Those dozy bucks that were bothering you earlier . . . they trade goods with the Maggitches. The bunch that's at permanent war with the Gurdles. That's why they were so scared of me. That, and one of them once had a disagreement with me . . . and my trusty hammer.'

'You knocked him out? Why?' Kree asked, giving the heavy hammer a wary look.

Coal leaned closer to the little plains rabbit and winked his good eye. 'He was saying rude things about the way I looked.'

Uki couldn't help but laugh at the expression on Kree's face. She was saved from squirming by the arrival of the gumbo.

It came in a big clay pot, steaming hot and smelling of sweetness and spices. It looked like a dark soup, filled with chunks of vegetable. Coal passed out some wooden bowls and ladled gumbo into them. When Uki tasted it, he blinked. It was fiery hot, with a pleasant warmth that tingled on his tongue. He spooned half the bowl into his mouth and savoured the layers of spice and sweetgrass.

'So,' he said to Coal, when his bowl was empty. 'Would you be able to guide some travellers around the fen?'

'Guide?' Coal gave the three of them a look, turning his head to take them all in with his remaining eye. 'What do you need to go there for? It's not a place for sightseeing. Not if you want to walk out again in one piece.'

Uki bit his tongue. He wasn't sure how much to tell this stranger. True, Coal had just helped them, but did that mean he could be trusted? Uki had been quick to confide in Jori and Kree when he met them – and that had been a good decision on both counts – but they were children, like him. Adults were much more . . . complicated.

'You don't need to know why,' said Jori. She spoke to Coal as if he was an equal, not a grown rabbit thirty years older than her. 'We can pay you. Two silver angels a day. In return, you will give us information on the fen and take us to these Gurdles.'

'Two angels? A day?' Coal rubbed his shredded ears with his hand. 'That's a handsome amount. Just for some guidance and information?'

Jori nodded. 'And no questions asked.'

Coal sighed. 'Very well. But I can't guarantee your safety once we're in the fen. The Gurdles will be all right with *me*, but they won't take kindly to outsiders like you coming in. If they decide to feed you to the adders, I won't be able to stop them.'

'We can look after ourselves,' said Kree, puffing out her chest again. She beamed at Uki, who cringed. He wasn't as invincible as Kree seemed to think. And he would much rather avoid fighting, even if he could punch a hole in an oak tree.

Coal sat back in his chair and used a claw to pick his teeth. 'Then what is it you brave explorers want to know?'

'The fen ... the plants, the animals. Have you noticed anything different lately?'

Coal was silent for a moment. Without fur, Uki could see the blood drain from his face, leaving him pale. When he spoke, his voice was quieter than before, more husky.

'Yes. Yes, I have. But how ... ?' He stopped, remembering Jori's instruction. 'There's been dead fish seen. Floating. And some of the wildlife has ... changed. Funny-looking eels. Diseased things. Dragonflies with two heads or too many wings. The Gurdles might be able to tell you more. Although they didn't want to speak about it with me when I tried. They just told me to make an offering to Lord Bandylegs. To ask him to take away the curse.'

'Who is Lord Bandylegs?' Jori asked. 'The head of their clan?'

Coal shook his head. 'No, he is their . . . I suppose you would say god. The story goes that he was once the Lord of Reedwic. Then, when the Empire was formed and Emperor Cinder ordered all Hulstland rabbits to forsake their gods and worship Kether, he refused. He was chased into the fen, where he stumbled into quickmud and was pulled under. The fen claimed him as its own and he became its guardian. Sometimes he appears as a rabbit with a ragged grey cloak and stilts. Other times he is a giant heron. His messengers are the dragonflies. They watch over the Gurdles and take their prayers back to him.'

'If the Gurdles don't believe in Kether, do they worship the Goddess?' Uki asked, thinking of his mother and her gentle beliefs.

Coal frowned. 'The Goddess? What does a little Hulstland kitten know of her?'

'I told you,' Jori interrupted. 'No questions.'

Coal's face creased into a smile again and he clapped his paw against his thigh. 'In that case, I recommend we share a cup of fen ale together before setting off to gather supplies. We can drink to our mysterious adventure.'

'Hooray!' Kree whooped, jumping up and down on her chair. Uki smiled, but paused when he caught Jori's eye. He was learning to read her expressions and this one said: *Uki, what have you done?*

CHAPTER FIVE

Bats and Bandages

'What supplies do we need, then?' Kree asked. 'It's not like we're climbing a mountain or something.'

They were outside the inn now, back in the bustle of the street. It made Uki nervous, being out here. Captain Needle and her Shrikes could be anywhere, watching them. **And what about Necripha and her Endwatch?** his dark voice added. **They could be out here too.**

No. Uki shook his head. *She couldn't have reached Reedwic so fast.* And as long as they got into the fen quickly, they had a good chance of losing her. She would need to find some kind of guide to follow them. Or perhaps she'd just charge in there, unprepared, and get swallowed in a bog. He silently crossed his fingers.

'Fresh water, for starters,' Coal was saying. 'The fen water is brackish in places, stagnant in others. Not good to drink. Then you'll all need walking staves. If we go off the paths, you'll have to prod ahead of you every step. There's patches of quickmud all over, and sometimes underwater holes. The Gurdles say they're bottomless.'

'I don't want to fall down a bottomless swamp-hole!' Kree was looking more and more upset with everything Coal said. The blacksmith, on the other hand, seemed to be enjoying himself immensely.

'You'll need rope, in case you have to pull someone out,' he continued, 'and some lavender or thyme oil. Keeps away the mosquitoes. And finally, if you have enough coin, Uki and Kree could do with some leather galoshes for their feet. Being wet and mud-caked for a long time can give you paw-rot.'

'What about Mooka?' Kree asked. 'Can you get galoshes for a jerboa?'

'Who or what is a Mooka?' Coal asked. Kree pulled him around to the stables and pointed out Mooka in his stall. He was nibbling oats and looking a little worried.

'You can't take *that* into the fen,' said Coal. 'They don't even have rats in there, let alone ... whatever he is.'

'He's a long-eared jerboa, and he's coming with us!' Kree crossed her arms and glared.

'I reckon Mooka will be fine,' said Uki. 'He's got long legs. Surely that will be good for wading?'

'The jerboa comes,' said Jori. 'And that's final.'

'Very well.' Coal shrugged. 'You're the bosses. Just don't ask me to pull it out of the mud when it gets stuck.'

Mooka looked at them with his huge brown eyes and gave a sad little *neek*.

*

They decided to split up, to save time. Uki still had half a purse of silver, left over from selling one of his crystal pieces in Nys, and he gave the others a few coins each. They spread out amongst the market stalls at the edge of the docks and went hunting for their supplies.

It was Uki's task to find the walking staves, and it didn't take him long to spot a stall full of woven baskets made from reeds and hazel twigs. There were also stacks of broomsticks, brushes and a tub full of lovely, straight staffs. Most of them had a 'v' at the top, formed by a natural fork in the wood.

A little old rabbit was sitting behind the stall, weaving a reed basket with nimble fingers. She looked up at Uki as he browsed and gave him a toothless smile.

'Can oi be helping you, young man?' (With her strong accent, it sounded like 'maaaaaaan', and for a moment, Uki wondered what she meant.)

'Yes, please. I need three walking staves. For going into the fen with.' Uki figured Coal would cope with his crutch, and besides, he wouldn't be able to hold one with his hammer-hand.

'There be some graaaand ones there,' the old rabbit said, nodding towards the tub.

'Why do they have a fork at the end?' Uki asked.

'That be for resting your thumb on,' said the rabbit. 'And, if'n you comes across a snake, you can trap it against the ground. If you be quick.'

Uki gulped. 'Are there many snakes?' he asked.

'Oh, squillions,' said the rabbit. 'Some gurt ones, the size of a longboat. Stick won't help you none if you run into one of *those*.'

Feeling even more nervous about his task than ever, Uki paid for the staves. The old rabbit tied them up with a piece of twine, and he started back to the inn, where they had agreed to meet.

As he wandered past the dock, he noticed a particularly splendid boat, just about to cast off with a full load of cargo. It was long and broad, the prow and stern sweeping up at either end and carved into the likeness of a dragon's head and tail. It had a single sail of red and white stripes, and flew a twisting silk pennant of deep purple from the mast.

Uki watched the sailor rabbits, dressed in brightly coloured tunics with broad leather belts and bandanas on their heads. They leaped about, throwing ropes and clambering rigging, not caring for an instant about all the cold, deep water around them. Uki wondered about their lives and how free they must feel, just sailing from one port to another, not having to chase after ancient spirits or hide from folk who wanted to kill you.

He was just imagining setting sail himself – heading out into the Endless Sea on a voyage around the coast, into Thrianta and beyond – when he felt someone grab hold of his spear harness and yank him backwards.

Too surprised to yell, Uki dropped his staves with a clatter. He was shoved into the gap between a market stall and a stack of wool bales, banging up against a wooden post. He looked up to see who had grabbed him and recognised the rabbit that had slipped out of the inn earlier. The one with the purple cloak.

'Don't make a sound,' the rabbit said. His eyes were narrowed, his lip curled. In one hand was a knife with a long thin blade.

'What do you want?' Uki asked. 'I have some money I can spare.' He had started to tremble, but then remembered his powers. If this rabbit made a move towards him with that knife, Uki could throw him halfway down the river.

'I don't want your money!' The cloaked rabbit spat at Uki's feet. 'I want *you*. You're the black-and-white rabbit the mistress is hunting.'

Mistress? Uki realised he meant Necripha. That old, three-eyed witch. She must have put word out, and this was one of her agents. As Uki watched, the rabbit took a squat wooden tube from his cloak. He pulled out the cork stopper with his teeth and shook the contents on to a wool bale beside him. A tiny curl of small brown fur. A mouse? A vole? The rabbit nudged it, and sleepy leather wings unfurled. *A bat.*

'Fly, curse you!' The rabbit flicked the poor creature, making it jump. Uki noticed a coloured ring had been clipped to one of its hind legs. It was shaking its bleary head, obviously distressed by the bright daylight. The rabbit flicked it again.

Uki realised he should probably stop the bat flying, but even as he started to reach out, it wobbled to the edge of the bale and fell off. There was a rustling, flapping sound, and it emerged from the other side, flying in mad spirals as it rose over the river. Uki watched it, willing it to fall or fly off in the wrong direction, but winced as it found its

CHAPTER SIX

The Perils of Frog Hunting

To get into the fen, they had to leave Reedwic and head west, following the river. They crept out of the gate, avoiding eye contact with the Shrike guards and keeping their ears pricked for Endwatch agents. Uki was glad to be out of the crowds of rabbits, not having to wonder who was spying on him and who to trust all the time. There was only the quiet bubble of the river on one side and the rolling fields on the other. Part of him wished they could just keep going like this, as if they were simply friends on a camping holiday. But he knew at some point they would have to turn off into the reeds and marshes, where he could sense the menacing presence of the spirit, pulsing like a boil under his skin.

Uki and Kree had new leather boots on their feet, squeaking and creaking. They were all, including Mooka, daubed in lavender oil, and as they marched they swung their staves in time. They looked like proper adventurers now, rather than a rag-tag gaggle of orphans playing make-believe heroes.

Finally, when Reedwic was out of sight around a bend in the river, Coal stopped them. He pointed to a log bridge that led across the water to a narrow earthen track on the other side.

'This is a good way in,' he said. 'Lots of paths this way. If you know where they are, you can almost get from one side of the fen to the other without even wetting your feet.'

'Is the Gurdle warren on one of these paths?' Uki asked. Despite his new galoshes, he wasn't looking forward to wading through a marsh. Especially after what that old rabbit at the market had said about snakes.

'On a path?' Coal laughed. 'It's not even on land.

The Gurdles live on boats and floating platforms made of roots and reeds. It's a moving village – in a different place every week. That's why the Shrikes can never find it.'

'How do *you* know where to find it, then?' Jori asked, giving Coal one of her looks.

'I don't. Not exactly.' Coal lifted his crutch and waved it in the direction of the fen. 'I know where it *has* been and where it *might* be. We just have to try a few places and see.'

'Call yourself a guide?' Kree glared at him as well. 'Even *I* could do that.'

'Not without getting yourself lost, you couldn't,' said Coal. 'Besides, it doesn't matter if we don't know the precise spot. The Gurdles will know we're coming long before we see them. If you're with *me*, they'll know you're trustworthy.'

There was a bit more grumbling, but Coal ignored it. He headed across the bridge, leaving them to follow. Uki paused for a moment, one foot on the log, one on the bank.

This is it, he told himself. *One more step and you're on the path again. And at the other end is*

Charice. It's not going to be easy, but it has to be done. Stop her, capture her and all the life in the Fenlands will be safe. You can do it, Uki. You have to. It's your task.

He nodded to himself, then balanced his way across, into the fen.

*

Uki had imagined wading through waist-high gloop. He had imagined clammy mud, sucking at his feet; hungry eels nibbling his toes. He had expected swarms of biting bugs, wisps of mist and a stench of damp, rotten ooze.

The Fenlands were nothing like that.

They walked along a narrow strip of bare earth. It was an old, old path, worn deep by many hundreds of tramping feet. There were little banks on either side, topped with tufty grass, and behind those were thick blackberry bushes and hawthorns. Beyond were seas of reed beds. Literally seas – they flowed in waves whenever the wind blew. Ripples of gold that swished along beside them with a quiet, soothing *hissssssssss*.

That sound was a constant background noise.

That, and the buzzing of dragonflies. They hummed everywhere – great, long darts with bulbous eyes and a shimmer of wings. Uki had never seen insects so big, or so colourful, and was hypnotised by the way they seemed to hang in the air before zipping sideways, or soaring up and over the nodding heads of the bulrushes to disappear into the distance. He stared after them as the sun gleamed on their shining bodies. Streaks of brilliant red, blue and green. It was hard to tell, but they didn't look warped or diseased, at least not in this part of the fen.

What a cruel thing, he thought. *To spoil such beautiful creatures.*

Imagine what it will do to rabbits, his dark voice added. **And the jerboas and rats and birds. Imagine what the world will look like when plague takes it all**.

Uki shuddered. He focused on the scenery around him, shutting that voice and its awful pictures out of his head.

There was lots of water. It flowed in a network of streams around them. In the distance were bigger ponds and lakes, with stretches of grass plain in between. They looked quite firm and dry, Uki thought, but then it *was* summertime. It was probably flooded for most of the winter. Perhaps it might even be the site of the floating Gurdle village, when the rains came.

They hadn't gone far when they saw their first heron. 'Look!' Kree, up on Mooka's back, had spotted it. 'It's Lord Bandylegs!'

And, Uki thought, it did look like a rabbit on stilts, wearing a shaggy grey cloak. Until it moved its head, stretching it upwards to reveal a long graceful neck and sharp orange beak. The cloak turned into a pair of wide, powerful wings, which it beat hard to take off, slapping sprays of water from the pool it had been standing in. Up and up it fought, until it was high enough to spread its wings and circle, keeping its eyes on the water below for tasty frogs and fish.

They carried on walking until the sun began to hang low in the sky and Uki noticed his stomach was rumbling. They hadn't stopped all afternoon, following one path or another, winding their way deeper into the fen, all without seeing a single soul. If it wasn't for the sickly presence of Charice at the back of his head, Uki might have thought this part of the world was completely deserted.

Jori must have been thinking the same thing as him. 'Are we getting closer?' she asked, keeping her voice low so Coal couldn't hear. Uki closed his eyes for a second and concentrated. Yes, the seething force of the spirit was definitely stronger now. A way off, but they were closing in.

'It's there,' Uki said, pointing to the south. 'Still quite far, but nearer than when we were in Reedwic.'

'We should think about setting up camp,' Coal said, interrupting Uki and making him jump. 'It'll be dark before long and we don't want to wander off the path.'

'Yes,' said Kree. 'Camp *and* supper. Uki's tummy is rumbling. I can hear it from up here.'

Uki blushed, but didn't deny it. It had been a long day and the chance to relax by a campfire would be more than welcome. Coal led them down from the path to where a gnarled, timeless oak tree stood, half of its roots spilling over the bank into a stream, the rest spread out in a web of twining wood dotted with acorn shells. Low branches hung almost to the ground, sheltering them from sight. It was the perfect spot to stop.

Kree and Jori began to gather twigs and dead branches for firewood, while Uki scooped out a fire pit with his paws. The earth was soft and crumbly and released a rich, damp, leafy smell as he dug into it. He was making it nice and deep, to hide the flames from unwanted eyes, when he heard a scream.

He looked up, ears pricked tall, searching for Kree and Jori. He quickly spotted them, not far away, their arms full of firewood. So who had made the noise?

'Trouble,' Coal said. 'Came from the other side of the path.'

Jori and Kree dashed over, setting their firewood down.

'We should go and see who it is,' said Uki. 'Someone might need help.'

Coal shook his head. 'It's best to ignore screams in the Fenlands,' he said. 'It could be anything from a Maggitch trap to a giant viper. Stick your nose in and you're likely to end up dead.'

The noise came again. It sounded like a young rabbit, shouting for help.

'I'm going,' said Uki. 'I have to.' He didn't have time to tell Coal about the bullying and torment he had suffered back in the Ice Wastes. He couldn't explain how he'd promised himself never to stand by while another rabbit was being picked on. Not now he had the power and the strength to *do* something about it.

'Come on!' Kree shouted, pulling her short spear from her bedroll. 'Let's go to the rescue!'

Coal groaned. 'I *really* don't think you should.'

'I agree,' said Jori. 'The last time we did this, we ended up with *her*, don't forget.' She gave Kree a wink and stuck out her tongue. Despite her words, she had already drawn her sword.

'At least wait for me,' Coal began to say, but they had already dashed off, leaving Mooka tied to the oak trunk.

They clambered back up to the path and followed it in the direction of the shouts. About twenty metres along, there was a gap in the bushes and a rough track leading down to one of the grassy floodplains. There, beside a broad, reed-lined pond, was a familiar red-armoured rabbit. Something small and furry squirmed in its grip.

'Shrike!' Jori hissed, diving into the cover of a blackberry bush. Uki and Kree skidded to a halt too, ducking down into the long, dry grass at the edge of the path.

'It's got someone,' Uki whispered. They could now see the Shrike was clutching a young rabbit – holding the poor thing up by the ears. It looked like a boy, with sandy brown fur and clothes made of patchwork leather tinged a muddy green. He had a wicker basket on a strap around his neck, from which a glistening frog's foot poked. His left leg was caught in a length of rope or wire, which trailed off to a wooden stake almost hidden in the reeds.

As they watched, the Shrike shook the boy hard, making him shout again. It waved the spikes on its right forearm in front of the terrified child's face.

'We have to stop this,' Uki said.

'There's only one of them.' Jori had her paw on the flask of dusk potion at her belt. 'At the moment, anyway.'

Uki put his paw over hers. 'I think I can take the Shrike on my own. Save your potion for now.'

'Be careful,' said Kree. She had her little spear at the ready, for all the good it would do.

'Look out for more soldiers,' said Uki. Taking a deep breath, he slipped out from cover and began making his way towards the Shrike as quickly and quietly as he could.

Ten, nine, eight metres. He ran on tiptoe, a rustle in the grass, lost in the constant whispering of the reeds.

As he got closer, he could hear the Shrike taunting the boy. 'You know what we do with poachers,' he was saying, his voice low and mean. 'We take them back to Bloodthorn. We put them on spikes. Right through their bodies. It takes them hours to die ...'

'Please,' the boy spoke through sobs. 'It was just a frog ...'

Uki could see his face twisted in pain as the Shrike gave his ears another jerk. Then he caught sight of Uki and his eyes widened in surprise. The Shrike saw the boy's expression change and turned round, just as Uki was closing the last couple of metres.

'What's this?' The Shrike dropped his prize and turned towards Uki, raising his arms, spikes pointing outwards. There was no need for him to draw a weapon with *those* at the ready.

'Leave that child alone,' said Uki, in what he hoped was a threatening growl. The Shrike laughed and stepped forwards, swinging his spiked right arm down and across in a blow that would have punctured Uki's chest.

If he hadn't seen it coming, that is.

Just like when he had been attacked in the twin cities, Uki's new senses seemed to wind down time. The sounds of the marshes fell away as the reeds stopped their endless waving. He could feel the slow beat of his heart, sense the power of the spirits filling every drop of his blood . . .

The Shrike's arm was drifting towards him at a crawl. The spikes twinkled, each needle-tip finely sharpened. Moving almost casually, Uki stepped aside and grabbed the Shrike's wrist with both hands. The armour was boiled leather, dyed and polished to a sheen. He could smell the lacquer and linseed oil. He could feel its smoothness and the muscles of the Shrike's arm underneath.

Then, dragging the arm with him, Uki stepped

sideways and swung himself around in a circle. The Shrike was yanked from his feet and hurled, like a hay bale or a sack of potatoes, up and over the pond, beyond the reeds on the far side, where it disappeared from view. As time snapped back to its normal speed, Uki heard a *crump*, followed by a howl of pain. And then silence.

Uki turned to see the young rabbit staring up at him, eyes wide. 'How . . . how did you do *that*?'

'Magic,' said Uki, smiling. 'Are you hurt?'

The young rabbit reached down to his leg, where a wire snare was cinched tightly round his ankle. It had cut through the fur into his skin and there was blood covering his foot.

'Well done, Uki!' Kree and Jori ran up, just as Uki was bending to inspect the rabbit's leg. He heard a familiar *clomp, clunk* and looked around to see Coal there too. He had been a few seconds behind, but in time to glimpse Uki throw the Shrike. His mouth was hanging open, wide enough for dragonflies to get caught inside.

'We need to cut this wire,' said Uki. 'Have we got anything to do that?'

'My sword is sharp,' said Jori, 'but it will take some time to cut through copper. Maybe we could pull the snare out at the stake?'

'I have some cutters.' Coal had scrambled down from the path and was hobbling over to them. 'But afterwards you're going to tell me how you did that.'

Jori crossed her arms. 'No questions, remember?'

Uki looked away. He didn't like hiding things, especially since Coal had been nothing but kind to them.

'Charcoal?' The wounded rabbit recognised Coal as he drew closer.

'Bo Gurdle? Is that you?' Coal shrugged his pack from his shoulders and began to rummage in it. 'Hold still. The more you move, the more the snare will tighten.'

'I was just ... catching frogs ...' The young rabbit – Bo – was trembling with the pain. His brown eyes showed whites all around. He looked like he was about to pass out.

'Here. Clippers.' Coal drew a small pair of bronze tongs from his bag. He moved to where Uki was holding Bo's leg and examined the snare. 'It's cut deep,' he said. 'It'll be tricky to get off.'

Just then, a sound of voices came from the far side of the pond. Angry voices and the clatter of armour. Every one of the rabbits pricked their ears and looked at each other, frightened.

'Sounds like there are more Shrikes,' said Jori.

'And they've found their flying friend,' added Kree.

'They'll be upon us before long,' said Coal. 'And I'd like to see you throw six or more into the swamp without getting spiked.'

The clattering sound of armour sounded again. The Shrikes had left their injured comrade behind to search the marsh. Coal was right: they didn't have much time.

All eyes turned to Uki, who blinked back, clueless.

'Well?' said Jori. 'What shall we do?'

The only thing Uki could think of was to pray.

CHAPTER SEVEN

Gurdle Gumbo

'Kree, how quickly can you run back and bring Mooka here?' After the first few moments of panic, an idea had begun to form in Uki's head.

'As quickly as a falcon,' said Kree, 'as she soars across the plains, swooping down like a bolt of lightning, on a mouse that has come out of its burrow to—'

'Just do it, will you?' Jori snapped. Kree stuck her tongue out, then scuttled off back to the path, keeping her ears low and out of sight.

'Bo.' Uki took the injured boy's paw and squeezed gently. 'Do you think you'd be able to guide us out of here? Back to your village?'

'I can't ... walk ...' Bo had his teeth gritted as Coal wiggled the wire about, trying to get a clean cut.

'Don't worry,' said Uki. 'We can give you a lift.'

'The Shrike are sure to spot Mooka,' said Jori. 'Perhaps we should try to attack them before they reach us. We could spread out and pick them off ...'

Uki shook his head. 'It's too dangerous. And they won't spot any of us if Bo can lead us through the reeds. He must know some secret pathways that the Shrikes don't.'

'Gurdles have more secret pathways than whiskers,' said Coal. There was a metallic *snip* as his clippers cut through the wire. He began to carefully peel it away from Bo's leg. The young rabbit winced as it came free and let out a yelp that he quickly stifled with his paws. Jori had a bandage at the ready, binding the wound clean and tight.

'I know it hurts,' whispered Uki. 'But can you try and tell us which way to go? The other Shrikes will be here any minute.'

Bo nodded and pointed along the pond's edge, following the line of reeds. As Uki began to gently lift up the injured rabbit, there was a scuffling sound on the path behind them. A great ball of fur on two spindly legs came bouncing through the long grass and down the bank, just as a shout went up nearby.

'I'm here!' Kree was clinging to Mooka's back, grinning wide and wild. 'I had to leave the staves and ropes behind, but I've got all our packs. We rode like the plains wind, but I think the Shrikes might have *just* seen me.'

'Here, take Bo!' Uki forgot about being gentle and tossed the little rabbit up to Kree as if he weighed no more than a heron feather.

'How ...' Coal began, but Uki was already moving, running along the reeds' edge in the direction Bo had shown them.

'Come on, old man,' Jori called, chasing after. Three or more armoured figures could be seen, gathering at the top of the bank and jostling to be the first to scramble down.

Mooka took off, speeding ahead of everyone with long, bouncing strides. Uki and Jori sprinted after, with poor Coal bringing up the rear, swinging his crutch and bounding as fast as he was able. His face was bright red with effort and his cheeks puffed out as he panted.

When they were nearly at the far end of the lake, Kree swung Mooka into the reeds, disappearing from sight. Uki and Jori reached the spot a few seconds later and pushed their way between the tall stalks. There was much shoving and stumbling as they fought their way through the thick plants to suddenly emerge at the very edge of the water. They saw Mooka, *neeking* with worry, while on his back Bo and Kree argued.

'What's the matter?' Uki asked. 'Why have we stopped?'

'He wants Mooka to go into the water, but there's snakes in there! I saw one swimming ... it was big enough to swallow us all whole!' Kree was holding the reins tight and almost shaking with fear.

'It were just a hopsnatcher ... a grass snake,' said Bo. 'We scared it off. Besides, we don't have to go *in* the water. There's stepping stones, just under the surface.'

'Whatever we're going to do, we have to be quick,' said Jori. 'Those Shrike will see the path we pushed through the reeds, and now we're backed up against this lake ...'

Uki stared where Bo was pointing. He could just make out – a few centimetres under the surface of the dark, soupy water – a round, solid object. A log, maybe, or a stone. There was no time to examine it further, to test if it was safe. He took a breath and leaped for it, landing with a splash and a skid ... and standing firm, the water only up to his ankles.

'Bo's right! Come on ... across the stones.'

Squinting to spot the next underwater platform, Uki hopped, hopped and hopped again. Behind him, he could hear splashes as the others followed. It didn't take long to cross the small lake and make it to the far bank, where a slight dent in the reeds hid what must be another secret path.

As soon as his feet were on solid land, Uki turned to watch his friends. Jori was only a single stepping stone behind him. He reached out and helped her make the last leap. Mooka was managing to land on each tiny platform with surprising accuracy, with

Kree gently talking him through every hop. Coal had caught up with them too and was halfway across, using his crutch as a kind of vaulting pole.

One by one, they reached the bank and disappeared into the safety of the reeds. Just in time, as the Shrikes burst through to the lake only seconds after Coal made his last jump. Peeping between the reed stalks, Uki saw them milling at the shore. They had seen the spot everyone had crossed to, but had no idea the stepping stones were there. They blundered up and down the bank for a few moments, until one of them was brave enough to step in. There was a huge splash and he sank down to his neck, floundering and waving his arms. Other ripples appeared in the water too, as things beneath the surface writhed and wriggled.

'Get me out!' the Shrike cried. 'There's things in here! I can feel them!'

His comrades all began reaching for him, trying to grab hold of his arms without spiking themselves, trying to haul him out of the sucking mud and filthy water. They toppled over each other, rolling in the reeds and getting covered with pondweed and green slime. It was all Uki could do not to burst out laughing. He watched for a few seconds more, and then turned to follow the others along the new path.

Twisting and turning through the bulrushes, they emerged into a patch of brackish, muddy water dotted here and there with tufts of grass and plants. It was brown and stagnant, with a swirling, patchy film covering its surface. Tiny things twitched and swam everywhere you looked. Uki could sense wisps of poison in the water. He knew if he bent close enough to stare at the little worms and larvae jiggling about, some of them would be swollen and blistered, choked up with plague and ready to pop. Every step deeper into the fen was taking them closer to Charice.

Uki didn't like the idea of wading through all that, and neither did any of the others judging by the looks on their faces, but Bo pointed out a series of dead tree logs, laid on their sides. They would be able to walk along them, like a bridge, keeping their feet clear of the unhealthy-looking water.

Stepping from one trunk to another, they were soon back up on a proper path, this one hidden from view by a series of weeping willow trees. They were all quite happy to have solid ground beneath their feet again.

'Thank you, Bo,' said Uki. 'Without you guiding us, those Shrikes would have caught us for certain.'

'Bain't no problem,' said Bo. 'You all saved my life back there. I's right grateful for it. Although how you got to be so strong is a muckle gurt mystery.'

'Yes,' Coal agreed. 'A mystery, indeed.'

Uki was flustered. Just how *did* you explain what had happened to him? Even when he'd told Jori and Kree, he'd been convinced they would laugh at him. Somehow, talking about it with an adult present seemed worse. In the end, all he could do was shrug.

Jori stepped in to rescue him from squirming. 'Perhaps we can tell you later. But for now, we would be very grateful if you could lead us to your village. We have important matters to discuss with your lord, or chieftain.'

'Lord?' Bo scratched his ear. 'Does you mean Ma Gurdle?'

'Yes,' said Coal. 'I was taking them to find her when we heard your shouts. They want to talk to her about what's happening in the fen.'

Bo rubbed his chin and looked thoughtful. He eyed Uki and the others up and down, giving Jori's sword and flask several worried glances. 'I don't know,' he said finally. 'We Gurdles don't like outsiders much. Ma might spank my bollycracker if I brings you lot in. Then again, you did save me, I suppose. And you are with Charcoal. Ma Gurdle trusts him.'

'Then you'll take us?' Uki asked. The sky was growing rapidly darker and he *really* didn't want to spend the night out in the wild fen with the snakes, frogs and whatever else might be lurking.

'I'll take you,' said Bo with a nod. 'But what happens to you when you gets there b'aint nothing to do with me.'

Uki let out a sigh of relief. Finding Coal, finding Bo ... it was almost like someone was looking out for them, making sure they got some of the help they needed. Which was just as well, considering all the forces that were trying to stop them.

Keeping a wary eye on the pools of water by the path, Uki followed behind Mooka, as Bo pointed the way.

*

They walked for another half hour, until night was almost upon them and all but the last glow of light had gone from the sky. Everything was reduced to grainy greyness, patched with deep shadows. Quiet noises filled Uki's ears: the fluttering wings of moths buffeting against the bushes; the gurgles and plops of creatures moving in the marsh; the high-pitched whine of mosquitoes as they buzzed past, searching for a juicy spot of bare skin.

Uki kept his eyes on the outline of Mooka, with Bo and Kree on his back. He followed their every step as they weaved this way and that along paths, through copses of trees and beside riverbanks. He marvelled at how Bo knew his way so well. If they had tried to come through here on their own, they would have been lost within minutes.

Just as the first stars began to appear in the sky, Bo tapped Kree on the back. 'Stop here,' he said. 'If we go any closer, they'll probably shoot you all.'

Everyone froze, scanning the murky darkness around them for Gurdle eyes. Uki couldn't see anything, let alone a secret village.

'Who goes there?' A cry came from somewhere up ahead.

'It's me! Bo!' The little rabbit raised himself up on Mooka's back and waved his arms. 'I was snaggled by the Spikers and these mudwalkers saved me. They want to talk to Ma!'

'Is that Charcoal with you?'

'It is!'

'And what's that big rat-thing?'

'I don't know!' Bo looked Mooka up and down. 'Some kind of giant hopping mouse?'

'What?!' Kree jabbed Bo in the back with a finger. 'He's a long-eared jerboa! The fastest thing on the plains! What is wrong with all you swamp rabbits?'

There was a long moment of silence, in which Uki imagined a swarm of arrows or spears, swishing their way through the gloom to pepper them all, Kree in particular. None came.

'Righto,' came the voice. 'Come on through. But keep yer hands off yer weapons!'

Bo gave them a nod and they set off again, walking towards what looked like a solid cloud of trees. Every now and then, Uki heard a rustle from the bushes beside the path, where things were hiding. Large things – rabbit-sized, he would say – and probably well armed. For the hundredth time that evening, he thanked his whiskers they were with Bo.

It was only as they were almost inside the treeline that Uki spotted the flicker of lanterns further on, peeping through the leaves. They kept walking, pushing through the curtains of dangling willow branches, and emerged at the edge of a wide lake. There, floating on the surface, sending ripples of golden light dancing across the water, was the Gurdle village.

It seemed like one sprawling jumble, but when he looked closer, Uki could see thirty or more boats, rafts and floating platforms all lashed together. Each one had some sort of structure on top, from tents and shacks to thatched cottages and even something that looked like a longhouse. Ropes were strung and looped between them all, tying masts and roofs together. Lanterns made of glass, clay and bone were hung along these guy ropes, illuminating everything with an orange glow. The whole place looked like one of the warrens they had just visited, decked

out for some kind of festival or party. Except, Uki realised, at the slightest sign of danger, the ropes could be cut and the boats and rafts would scatter into the maze of rivers and waterways that made up the fen. It was a village that could literally disappear.

With the light from the lanterns, Uki could now see a ring of armed sentries standing on the banks around the floating settlement. They had the same short ears and sandy fur as Bo, the same long legs and oversized feet, and they were dressed in clothes made from that green-brown leather. *Frogskin*, Uki remembered, from what Jori had told him. They were all carrying bows, spears and clubs, some tipped with sharp barbs that looked as if they might be snakes' fangs. They looked fierce, defensive ... but they were just rabbits, the same as everyone else. Uki wondered why Father Klepper and the Shrikes hated the Gurdle rabbits so much.

Every eye was trained on the newcomers as they stepped from the bank on to the wooden walkway that led into the village. When he looked up, Uki could see other rabbits on the rooftops and perched in the masts. More than one of them had their bowstrings pulled taut, arrows ready to fly. Coal hadn't been exaggerating when he said these rabbits hated outsiders.

'Ma's house is the big one in the middle,' Bo said. With some help from Jori, he slid down from Mooka's back and began to walk in front, limping as he went. 'She'll be sitting in the square. Tonight's the Feast of Gollop. That's what all the lights is for.'

The planks of the walkway reached a wide-bottomed boat that served as the village entrance, and then continued, winding their way between the boats like a path or road. Bo led them in between the tents and houses, turning this way and that. Apart from each footstep causing a gentle rocking, it was just like having a stroll through any other little town.

They passed from boat to boat until they came to an enormous floating platform. It seemed to be made from mats of living roots, twisting in, out and over each other. Logs, moss and planks of wood were mixed in – buried, twined or nailed in place. Some looked fresh, others old and rotten. It was obvious this thing had been around for many years, added to and expanded over time.

At one end was the thatched longhouse, with its double doors flung wide open. A fire blazed in front of it, the burning logs stacked inside a wide copper plate, raised off the ground on legs. Several rabbits sat around it, watching nervously for stray coals. Bonfires on wooden boats weren't the safest of things.

There were flagpoles all around the edge of the platform, strung with hundreds of lanterns. In between stood lots of rabbits, wary eyes staring at the intruders. And, on a throne-like wicker chair before the longhouse, sat a grand rabbit, who was watching them closest of all.

She wore a long grey cloak made of heron feathers, robes of patched frogskin and a necklace of curved viper fangs. Her eyes were the deep brown of swamp pools, milky around the edges with age. In one hand she held a staff, carved into the shape of a heron, with a long, elegant beak and a plume of feathers at the back. Her other hand trailed over the arm of her chair to rest upon the head of the biggest frog Uki had ever seen. It was the size of an adult rabbit at least, crouched so motionless he thought it must be a statue. That is, until a bright pink tongue slipped out of its mouth to lick one of its golden eyes.

'Ma,' said Bo, bowing his head. Jori and Coal copied him, Uki joining in a second later. Everyone seemed to be waiting for her to speak, until the silence was interrupted by a shout from one of the rabbits standing beside her.

'Bo! Where have you been?' A lady rabbit with a brown cloak and frogskin dress ran out to grab their new friend. She hugged him hard and then gave his shoulders a quick shake. 'How dare you stay out all this time! Don't you know how worried your pa and I have been? And what's happened to your leg?'

Bo held out his injured foot for all to see. 'I was off catching hoppets – got a good one here, see – when I got stuck in a Spiker's snare. One of those old redshells came along and nearly pulled me ears off. He was going to take me back to Bloodthorn and spike me, then these folk turned up and walloped him.'

'Is this true?' Bo's mother asked, looking at Uki and the others.

'He's taken quite a nasty wound from the snare,' said Jori. 'I've bound it, but it will need proper cleaning. Maybe some stitches.'

Bo's mother gave him another quick hug, then bobbed her head to Jori. 'Thank 'ee,' she said, before dragging her son off with her. Uki hoped it wasn't to spank his bollycracker.

There was a murmuring from all the Gurdle rabbits around the square. Uki watched them from the corner of his eyes, trying to judge their mood. Surely saving Bo would get them in the tribe's good books?

Ma Gurdle stared at them a few moments more as the mumbles and whispers went on. When she cleared her throat, the silence was instant.

'It seems,' she said, 'that we owe you our thanks. We don't often allow outsiders in here. Don't trust 'em, see. But you folk *might* be allowed to stay for the night. Once we's had a little chin-waggle.'

'Does that include me?' Coal asked.

'Oh, indeed it do, Mister Smith.' Ma fixed him

with a look of iron. 'I'd like to know how you come to be back here, with these young mollygogglers in tow.'

'If you please, ma'am.' Uki surprised even himself by speaking up, but he didn't want Coal to get in trouble. 'We paid him to guide us. We wanted to meet you, to ask you some questions about what's happening in the fen.'

'What's happening around here don't be no business of yours, little maggety-pie.' Ma squinted her eyes at Uki, then Kree, then Jori. 'You there, with the big slicer and the silver bottle. Are you one of them Duskers from up north?'

'I am,' said Jori, bowing slightly.

'And is it happening that you lot is hate-feuding with those redshell Spikers, those glommating wazzocks, the Shrikes?'

'Our clans have been opposed to each other for many years, yes.'

'That's good to hear. Nothing like a good hate-feud to keep your blood boiling.' Ma gave Jori a nod, as if she had been approved. 'And you, tiny painted rabbit. Is that beast you're sitting on a . . .'

'HE'S A—' Kree began to shout the words, but

Jori swiftly reached up and clapped a hand over her mouth.

'. . . a long-eared jerboa?' Ma Gurdle finished. 'The chosen mount of the Kalaan Klaa?'

'How . . . how did you know that?' Kree asked, from between Jori's fingers.

'I've travelled the Blood Plains,' said Ma. 'Many a moon ago now, when I was but a spratty mollygoggler myself. Nearly married the chief of an Uluk Miniki tribe. Until I realised they was all pikenoddling paddlewhackers. Almost as bad as them Maggitch scum.'

'Yes!' Kree punched the air. 'The Kalaan Klaa hate the Minikis! At least, I think we did the last time I was there. We might be blood brothers now. It changes quite a lot.'

All these rabbits that hate each other, Uki thought. *Don't they realise they're all the same underneath the fur?* It seemed so stupid to him, being caught up in all that rage and fighting. Such a waste of their lives, especially when there were *real* problems to deal with. Actual ancient evils that wanted to wipe all rabbitkind from existence.

You hated those bullies, his dark voice reminded him. **You even wanted to hurt them, for what they did to your mother.**

But he hadn't. Even though he'd had the power to. And when he set his anger aside, it was like a boulder had dropped from his shoulders. Like his soul had become light again. If these other rabbits could only see that their feuds hurt themselves more than anybody … but he was just a child; unwanted, even by his own tribe. Who would listen to him?

'And you, there.' Ma Gurdle was squinting at him now. 'Mister jumbled-eyes. Stitched-together thing. What's your story?'

Here goes, he thought.

'I'm nothing special,' he said. 'I'm not a fighter or a rider or a smith, like my friends. But I do have a quest. There's something bad in the fen – you might have seen creatures it has sickened or poisoned – and I am here to stop it. We know the cause of it all is somewhere nearby. We wanted to speak to you, to see if you knew exactly where, and if you might be able to take us to it.'

There was a long silence as Ma Gurdle stared at Uki. The only sound was the crackle of the fire and the occasional *slurp* as her giant frog licked its eyeballs. Just when Uki thought they might be standing there all night, Ma gave her head a slight shake. Her mind being made up, she began to speak.

'It is true. There is a wrongness in the Fenlands. Everyone here has seen it.' There came a murmur of agreement from all the gathered Gurdles. 'And I *can* tell you where it comes from. We all knows that as well.'

'It's them Maggitches!' shouted a Gurdle on the far side of the fire.

'Bandylegs curse them!' called another.

'Hushen up!' Ma Gurdle thumped her staff on the rooty floor. The voices instantly stopped. She turned back to Uki. 'Yes, it's the Maggitch family. Those snake-loving sneaks what live to the south. I expect Charcoal has told you about them and us. All the hating and fighting. Well, this time they's gone too far. They's done something to anger Gollop, and she's put a hex on them. *That's* what the wrongness is. It's their curse, spreading out from them and into everything they touch.'

'But . . .' Uki began to say. 'But it isn't . . .'

'Don't you dare naysay me!' Ma Gurdle banged her staff again and Uki saw a glimpse of the raw fury in her eyes. The fiery hatred that had let her spend a lifetime loathing another family for reasons that were probably long forgotten. 'I'm telling you now. Gollop has put her curse on them, and it's hers to take away. You're all welcome to stay for the night as thanks for saving our Bo, but the ways of the fen are not yours to meddle in. The curse will run its course.'

Ma Gurdle sat back in her chair and closed her eyes, which seemed to signal the meeting was over. The rabbits around the fire began to mill about and some sat down to play their long-necked lutes. Soon, music filled the night air and the floor of the Gurdle village began to gently rock as the rabbits danced and sang.

Uki and the others wandered across to the edge of the raft, sitting down on some crates that had been stacked there. Uki looked out past the village to where the surface of the lake reflected all the flames and lanterns back at him in wavy patterns of gold light.

'Don't worry,' said Coal. 'It's incredibly tough to get through to these Gurdles. We can try again in the morning. Perhaps she'll come around.'

Uki sighed. They were so close. Charice could have taken control of a Maggitch, but it would be almost impossible to find her in the maze-like fens, let alone capture her with one of his spears. And all because of a stupid feud.

'Who is this Gollop anyway?' Jori asked. 'Some kind of god?'

'She's *the* god,' said Coal. 'Around here, anyway. They believe she was about before Bandylegs. Before the old goddesses, even. She's a giant frog and she dug out the Fenlands herself with her webbed feet. They reckon she can still be seen sometimes, swimming in Toadtwitch Lake. The mist is her breath, the thunder her croaks . . . the usual old gubbins.'

'Can we find the Maggitches on our own?' Uki asked. 'Do you know where they might be?'

Coal twitched what was left of his ears. 'All I know is that their territory is to the south. I've heard rumours that they have a warren on Gollop's Mound, which is a hill a few miles from here. But they would shoot me on sight. You too, probably. They're even harder to get on with than the Gurdles.'

Uki turned his head, sensing the pulsing evil of Charice. It was indeed coming from the south, but it might as well have been on the other side of the world.

A rabbit came over to them with some bowls of gumbo and a jug of ale, but Uki no longer felt hungry.

He watched the folk around him dancing and singing, as if they had no cares at all. Even Kree and Coal were tapping their feet and nodding their heads. And yet, in the very water under their feet, there were signs of things changing. Evil was seeping out from the heart of the fen, where Charice was brewing something terrible. Uki could feel it in his bones, even as the music played; each note, each beat counting them closer to the end of everything, and no one seemed to care except him.

INTERLUDE

The bard stops there and takes a swig from his waterskin. All day long, the tale has gone on and now the tower room has begun to grow dark again, shadows stretching out and seeping into each other. From her perch by the blocked doorway, Jori pokes her nose out to spy on their besiegers.

'They've lit their fire again,' she says. 'Looks like they're settling in for the night.'

'Perhaps we can have a fire too,' says the bard. 'I think my story is done for the day. My voice won't hold out much longer.'

'Can't you please go on?' Rue asks. 'Just a bit after supper?'

The bard shakes his head. 'Let's save it for tomorrow. It's a good way to kill the time and we have nothing else to do but wait.'

Rue pouts a little, but nods. 'You were right, earlier. It has made me feel a lot better,' he says. 'Uki was a bit like me. He had rabbits wanting to hurt him, but he had to be brave about it. Jori and Kree too, of course.'

'It was a scary time,' said Jori. 'And we *were* just children like you, Rue. But you don't get any less scared as you get older, unfortunately.'

'Really?' Rue's eyes widen in surprise. 'Are you scared now, then?'

'Of course. Being brave doesn't mean you aren't frightened. It just means you carry on with what you have to do in spite of it. You get the job done, even though you feel like running away and hiding in a burrow somewhere.'

Rue thinks about this for a moment as the bard goes about kindling a small fire and rationing out their food for supper. It's a good few minutes before he speaks again.

'It's funny how stories can do that, isn't it? Make

135

you feel better, I mean. I was terrified before, but hearing about how Uki had to be strong . . . I feel like I can be strong now too.'

'That's what tales are for,' the bard agrees. 'They can pass the time, they can hand down history, but most of all they can show us that other rabbits go through the same things as us. Stories tell us that we're not alone. Every thought and feeling you've ever had has been thought and felt before.'

'We're all part of the same story,' says Rue. 'The story of all rabbits.'

'*That*,' says the bard, smiling, 'is something a true bard would say.'

*

Night falls quickly after they eat and Rue curls up in his cloak by the fire to sleep again. It's surprising how tired he feels, even after doing nothing all day. The crackle of the flames soon lulls him to sleep and he welcomes it, imagining Jaxom dashing towards them with a rescue party, his jerboas leaping across the foothills.

At some point in the early hours, Rue dreams a terrible nightmare. He is in the tower, being hunted by one of the swamp snakes. An enormous, coiled thing, dripping with slime. Its red eyes glow and its mouth yawns open, showing metal fangs the size and shape of Jori's sword.

Its head tracks Rue wherever he moves until it leaps, shooting out at him like an arrow. Those fangs jab into Rue's chest, just above his heart, punching into him with a deafening *snap*!

Rue jolts awake, kicking himself out of his cloak, and lies there panting. It takes a moment for him to realise he's still in the tower, but that the snake isn't real. The snapping sound was just the fire, the serpent just a shadow from the bard's story. Breathing slowly, he waits for his little heart to stop hammering so hard against his ribs.

'Bad dream?'

Sitting up, Rue sees Jori, still at the doorway, still staring out towards the Endwatchers.

'Just a bit,' says Rue. 'Are you going to stay awake all night?'

'For a few hours more. Then it'll be Pookingford's turn.'

'He told you his real name?'

'Oh, I've always known.' Jori sniggers. 'When did you find out?'

'At the end of our last adventure,' says Rue. 'When I discovered he was *in* the Podkin story.' He looks over to where the bard is snoring, unable to hear what they are saying, thank the Goddess.

'Well, don't tell anyone else,' says Jori. 'Not if you value your tail. Now, go back to sleep, little one. Nothing will hurt you while I'm here.'

Rue nods and snuggles back up in his cloak. Knowing Jori is there, with her sword and dusk potion, makes him feel as safe as he ever did, back in his own bed in his own warren.

*

When Rue awakes, the bard is just clambering down from the rubble after finishing his watch. Jori has a pot of water on the boil and is adding herbs to make tea.

'Morning, sleepyhead,' she says.

'Are the Endwatchers still there?' Rue asks, rubbing his gritty eyes.

'I'm afraid so,' says the bard. 'And no sign of rescue yet. It's going to be another long day.'

'Good job there's lots of Uki's story left to tell,' says Rue. He still has the lingering image of that terrible snake in his head and would like to have his mind taken off it.

'Yes, good job indeed,' says the bard, rolling his eyes. 'But can I have my tea first? I've only had a few hours' sleep, you know.'

'You can talk while you're drinking,' says Rue. 'Help could be here any minute and I want to find out what happens first.'

'You're a hard master,' says the bard, secretly happy to have such a keen audience. He takes his seat by the fire. Jori hands him a cup of tea, and he takes a quick sip before beginning Uki's tale once more.

CHAPTER EIGHT

Swarm

'Gollop's big and Gollop's wide,
Her bollycracker's a mountainside.
Gollop's big and Gollop's strong,
Her fat pink tongue is ten miles long.'

As the night wore on, there was no sign of the singing
and dancing even beginning to wind down. Uki had
moved to the edge of the platform, as far away as
possible from all the prancing and yodelling. Even
so, there was a Gurdle with one of those twangy lutes
perched on a root just a few metres away, singing
about Gollop at the top of his voice.

Uki sighed.

Kree was over on the other side of the platform, giving young rabbits rides on Mooka's back. Coal had left him a while ago. Uki glimpsed him here and there, talking to rabbits, looking at the edges of blades and metal tools they showed him, or just chatting and laughing. Even Jori had wandered off. He could see her by the grog table with a boy who looked about the same age as her. Much older than Uki, anyway. It made an uncomfortable knot of bad temper bubble under his skin and he wasn't sure why. He wasn't even sure who he was angry at. The boy for talking to his friend? Jori for not staying by his side? Himself for not being out there like everyone else, having fun and laughing?

It was all so confusing. Things were never this way when it was just him and his mother. There hadn't ever been any other rabbits around to complicate things. In fact, he realised, this was the first time he'd ever been to a party of any kind. He had no idea what he should be doing, how he should behave.

Mother. She would have loved to be here, to see this. She always talked about life in the rest of the

Five Realms. About all the things they could see together, once they had escaped the Ice Wastes. If only she could be here now, beside him. Then this terrible loneliness might go away.

Thinking of his mother, missing her … it made him feel like the lake they were floating on. Lights sparkled on the surface – life went on – but underneath it was dark and cold and bottomless. His sadness felt like that now. Like it would never end, just sink down and down forever.

'That's a very glum face you're wearing.' Uki looked up, to see Coal. The blacksmith had somehow managed to make his way over to him while holding two cups in his good hand *and* using his crutch. He had a lazy, lopsided smile on his face, which made Uki think he might have had a bit too much grog to drink.

'Sorry,' Uki said. 'I don't really know what to do at parties.'

'You don't?' Coal handed him a cup and then tumbled himself down on to the root next to Uki, nearly knocking him into the lake in the process. 'Don't they have parties where you come from?'

Uki thought back to his days in the tribe. There had been celebrations, he supposed, but as an outcast he had never been allowed near them. 'I guess they did. But I was never invited.'

'Really? A handsome chap like you?' Coal belched so hard the raft rocked up and down. 'Why was that?'

Uki pointed to his different-coloured eyes and the two halves of his fur. 'They didn't like the way I looked,' he said. 'They thought I was a demon.'

Coal blinked a few times, then let out a huge, husky bellow of a laugh. 'A demon? You? You're the cutest demon *I've* ever seen! Imagine if they got a look at me? *That* would make them run for the hills!'

Uki couldn't help laughing as well. To hear Coal describe it, it *was* a bit ridiculous.

'Doesn't it bother you?' Uki asked, when he'd stopped chuckling. 'The things rabbits say about you?'

'It used to,' Coal said. He looked out at the lake and, as Uki had been doing, seemed to see back into his past. 'It used to bother me a lot. Made me doubt myself. Made me think it must be true.'

His eye began to well up, but then he gave his head a hard shake and laughed again. 'Damn lake,' he said. 'Making me go all thoughtful and melancholy. Something about looking out at the night water like that. All peaceful and mysterious, eh?'

Uki nodded. It wasn't the best thing to do when you had lots of worries on your mind.

'The thing is,' said Coal, waving his cup in the air, 'you can't let them get to you. All those rabbits with mean words to say ... they have no idea who you *really* are, do they? They just see somebody different to them, and it scares them. Then they get angry for being scared and take it out on you. It's the sort of thing little kittens do in the warren playburrows. They're like babies, the lot of them. You and I, we can rise above, can't we? We know it's what's inside that counts.'

'A good heart and kind thoughts,' said Uki, remembering what his mother used to say.

'Yes.' Coal looked at him, almost looked *through* him. 'Yes. That's right. My heart hasn't always been good, or my thoughts kind. But I would like them to be. I would like that very much.'

144

A silence fell between them then, and the sounds of the singing and dancing seemed to grow distant. Uki found he liked the company of this old, scarred rabbit. Despite what Jori might say, he didn't want him to wander off again. And he wanted to show that he trusted him ... that he was more than just a paid guide.

'Coal,' he said. 'If you'd like to know, I can tell you about my quest. About why we're here in the Fenlands, and how I was able to throw that Shrike around.'

'Really?' Coal gave a hiccup, his head swaying as he tried to keep Uki in focus. 'That would be good of you. If you're sure I can be trusted.'

'I'm sure,' said Uki. And he began his tale, from the moment he woke up in the graveyard to the day they arrived in Reedwic, following the trail of Charice.

Coal listened intently to every word, stifling the odd burp with the back of his hand. His eye barely blinked as he heard all about Valkus and Gaunch, and how the spirits were trapped in the crystals on Uki's harness.

'Is that them?' he asked in a whisper, as Uki's tale finished. 'Is that the spirits, glowing in those crystals?'

'It is,' said Uki. 'And there is space for two more. I need to trap Charice and then Mortix. If I don't, the whole world could end.'

Coal let out a low whistle and scratched at one of his ragged ears. 'Now *that* is a story and no mistake. A proper legend happening right here and now. No wonder you were wary about trusting me, what with this Endwatch and everyone else after you.'

Uki nodded. 'I'm glad you believe me,' he said. 'I'm sorry we couldn't tell you sooner. And I'm sorry for any danger we might have put you in.'

'Danger? Don't you worry about that.' Coal clinked his cup with the one Uki still clutched in his paw. 'It's an honour to be a part of something like this. A chance at being a real hero, instead of just a blown-apart blacksmith, hobbling around Hulstland.'

'A part of it? You mean you're not scared?'

Coal laughed again. 'Scared? Probably. Who wouldn't be? But I'll not be running off and leaving you. I said I'd get you to where you wanted to go and I meant it. Besides ... I'd like to see how this all plays out. Maybe one day there'll be a bard telling a tale about me, or singing my name in a song.'

Uki smiled. He hadn't really thought about tales and songs. All he wanted to do was complete Iffrit's task. To keep everyone safe from the evils he had seen in his visions. How strange that rabbits might remember him for what he'd done. **Supposing you survive,** his dark voice added. **Let's not forget about that.**

He was about to answer himself with a few stern words, when there was a commotion from the rabbits gathered around the fire. Shouts and screams, very different to the raucous noises he had been hearing. Voices tinged with unmistakable panic.

'Sounds like trouble,' said Coal, standing up with the help of his crutch.

Uki leaped up too, but was hit by such a powerful throbbing in his head, he nearly collapsed again. 'Charice ...' he managed to gasp. 'It's her ... she's here!'

Caught up with all his worries, he hadn't felt the creeping rise of sickness. Not until it was too late – not until she was practically on top of him. But there was no mistaking it. His every sense was blaring out her presence ... she was in the Gurdle village somewhere, only metres away!

He reached behind his head, grabbing a spear from his harness. Even as he began to focus, to try and pinpoint the spirit in all the noise around him, there was a loud *whooshing* sound from the bonfire in the platform's centre. Some substance had been thrown into the flames, making a mushroom cloud of smoke billow out. Green and stinking, the fumes rushed over the whole village in an instant, making every rabbit stagger and cough.

'Attack! Attack!' Alarm cries went up from the roofs, the banks, everywhere. 'It's the Maggitches! Maggitch attack!'

Uki ran forwards, towards the glow of the bonfire. He could sense Coal next to him, hammer arm outstretched and ready to strike.

'Uki! Where are you?' a voice called out nearby, and suddenly Jori was there, wrapping her arms about him in a tight hug. 'Thank Kether! I couldn't find you! I got stuck talking to that stupid, boring boy and then there were screams and smoke ...'

'It's Charice!' Uki shouted. 'She's here, in the village!'

'Whiskers!' Jori drew her sword and stared about her, trying to squint through the smoke. 'Where's Kree? Where's Mooka?'

Clutching arms, they moved forwards, Coal close beside them. Forms surged from the smoke, making them jump, but they were always just Gurdle rabbits, fleeing from the attack, trying to get somewhere safe. It was only when they reached the other side of the fire that they saw the figures.

As the stinking green fumes began to ebb, they could make out a group of rabbits standing at the platform edge. Cloaked and hunched, their silhouettes seemed wrong somehow . . . bulging and unbalanced. Unlike any rabbits Uki had seen before. There were five or more, all draped in hooded cloaks of shiny leather. Squares of scaled skin, patterned with black zigzags. The capes hung low over their bodies and faces, almost hiding the tortured forms underneath.

Almost.

As Uki stared, the tendrils of smoke parted and the invaders came into focus.

Plague. Rot. Virus. These rabbits had been ravaged by all three. Uki could see scraps of sandy fur and the long, splayed toes of the other fen natives, but they were the only traces of the creatures these things had once been. Charice's touch had been cruel. Now their eyes were swollen, sealed shut with crusted pus. Mucus dripped from their nostrils, dribbled from their open mouths. Every scrap of flesh was blistered and raw, covered in layers of boils and sores that hung in bunches, hiding their paws or burying their necks in ripples of bulging tissue.

'I think ... I think that's Granny Maggitch ...' Coal pointed with his hammer at the figure in the centre. His paw was clamped over his mouth, trying to block out the sweet, sickening stench of disease that was now even stronger than the smoking fire.

'*Pok ha boc!* What is wrong with those rabbits?' Kree had found them, dragging a coughing Mooka behind her. But Uki didn't have time to welcome her. He was too busy staring at the figure in the middle of the huddle. The thing that Coal had said was Granny, the leader of the Maggitch clan.

Just like when he had come face to face with

Valkus in the body of Mayor Renard, Uki was seeing two things at once. One was the solid, poisoned body of an old she-rabbit, the other was the ghostly image of Charice, spirit of plague and disease, floating in front of Granny's hunched form like a mirage.

The senses he had absorbed from Iffrit let him see her true form when no one else could. A tall, thin, earless creature with thin strands of hair straggling from her head. More corpse than anything, her leathery skin was pocked and scarred with the ravages of countless diseases. Her yellowed eyes were blind and blank, yet glowing with cruel power at the same time.

He recognised her instantly from memories the fire guardian had shared with him, from the countless centuries that Iffrit had circled above her, imprisoned on an island where she had built a poison workshop to brew her vile diseases. He knew she had been made by the Ancients to help fight sickness, but had instead fallen in love with the plagues she was supposed to cure. He knew she wanted to fill the world with her viruses, choking everything except those she chose to follow her, their minds clouded by the germs that swirled through them. An army of half-dead rotten things, forced to worship her against their will, even as they crumbled to pieces.

'Quick, Uki.' Jori squeezed his arm, her jaw clenched as she fought back the wave of nausea that swept over her. 'Your spear . . .'

Uki shook his head clear of his visions and raised the spear, ready to throw it into Charice's heart and trap her forever in its crystal head.

He wound back his arm, just as the possessed body of Granny Maggitch opened its mouth and bellowed: 'Gurdles! I bring a gift to end our petty squabbles once and for all! I bring you perfect plague! I bring you delectable disease!'

Before Uki could release the spear, there came a roaring, hissing sound. Loud enough to make him wince, it built up from somewhere in the swamp behind, then rushed towards them, shaking the matted wood of the platform, making the lanterns dance on the ropes above them.

And then, like a tsunami wave crashing on to a beach, a solid black cloud of buzzing, chittering insects blew out of the trees, engulfing the Gurdle village, smashing towards Uki and his friends as fast as a thunderclap.

They had an instant in which they could make out countless thousands of insect bodies, plates of shiny chitin and glimmering wings, and then the swarm was upon them. Uki felt a shove, throwing his aim off as Coal stepped in front to shield him. There was a *smack* as the wall of bugs hit him, and then they were up and over, covering Uki from head to toe and making the smith's brave gesture pointless.

Biting, crawling, stinging, Uki could feel them on every exposed part of his fur. He screwed his eyes shut and curled into a ball, trying to keep the insects off him. Still, they crawled up his sleeves and trouser legs, into his galoshes, between his toes. Every time they sank their mandibles into him it burned and, judging by the screams from all around him, it was the same for the others.

The stinging seemed to last for hours, although it was probably just a matter of seconds. As fast as they had come upon them, the horde of bugs moved on. They poured over the Gurdle village and then vanished, most of them falling into the swamp, their

fragile wings torn to shreds, their bodies cracked and broken by all the poisons they carried.

Free of the biting creatures, Uki scrambled to his feet. He lifted his spear again, trembling with the effort as his body used every scrap of its strength to fight off the toxins that had been injected into him.

'Charice . . .' he croaked, looking for the hooded rabbit again, hoping that he could make all this sickness vanish with one well-placed shot.

But there was no sign of her, or the other Maggitches. Like their swarm of insects, they had vanished, leaving desolation behind them. Every single rabbit in the village lay curled on the floor, gasping and twitching. Drifts of dead bugs were swept against walls and doorways like some kind of black, glittering snow. The music had stopped, the dancing had finished.

Plague had come and snuffed out the Gurdles like a candle.

CHAPTER NINE

Last Words

'Please don't die.'

Uki whispered the words to Jori as he held a damp cloth to her mouth. He squeezed out a few drops of water and she made a weak attempt to swallow them. Gently, Uki laid her head back down and watched her eyelids flutter as she fought to breathe. She was worse than she had been ten minutes ago and there was absolutely nothing he could do to help her.

Fighting back tears, Uki clenched his fists until it hurt, then looked down at his useless paws. What good was all his strength and power now? If only he had thrown that spear quicker ... If only he had sensed Charice before she arrived in the village ...

This was all his fault. Jori, Kree, Coal ... they wouldn't even be here if it wasn't for him.

Stop feeling sorry for yourself. His dark voice, normally cruel and mocking, talked sense for once. **Crying and whimpering won't help. Do what you can. That's all there is. Water. Comfort. Care.**

Uki nodded. Picking up his cloth and bucket, he started another round of tending to the dying.

*

After the attack, after the insects had crashed over them all, Uki had been in great pain. His body had been covered in lumps and bites – angry red bumps pushing through his fur all over. His eyes swollen shut, his skin burning like fire. Through the itching and stinging, he had been aware of cries and moans all around him. Every other rabbit in the Gurdle village must have been caught in the attack. They were all feeling the same pain.

But the others didn't have an ancient spirit fused with their body. After the longest hour of his life, just as Uki thought he might go mad from the hundreds of blistering stings, the pain had begun to ease a bit.

A few minutes later and he had been able to sit up. He'd prised his gummed eyes open and looked at his paws and arms. The bites had begun to fade away, his flesh shrinking back to normal. He had been able to feel his body wiping out the toxins: soothing, cleansing. Soon, every last itch had gone and the absence of hurting was like plunging into a cool, clear lake. It had been bliss.

And then he'd looked around.

There wasn't a single rabbit left standing. Curled in balls, huddled against each other, the Gurdles and his friends had all been hit by the bugs. Bitten all over, just like him.

That was when Uki had noticed the silence. All the moans and cries had stopped, which, unlike in his case, wasn't a good thing.

Terrified at what he might find, Uki had peeled back Jori's cloak and rolled her over. And what he saw almost made him scream. He would not have recognised his friend if it hadn't been for the black tips of her ears. Her whole face, neck, paws ... everything was swollen with thousands upon thousands of bites. It looked like someone had shoved bunches of grapes under her skin.

Moving closer, Uki had listened hard for any signs of life, praying to the Goddess that there were some. As he'd rested an ear next to her mouth, he had been rewarded by a faint tickle of breath.

Jori was alive. Just.

When he had done what he could to make her more comfortable, Uki had begun the process of checking the others. Kree and Coal were still unconscious, but breathing. Even Mooka had been knocked out by the attack.

Not knowing what else to do, Uki had gone around the village, picking up the Gurdles and bringing them on to the platform. He found Ma Gurdle, half buried in a mountain of dead bugs. Her giant frog was nowhere to be seen – Uki guessed it had sensed the wave of insects coming and jumped into the lake to escape. If only the rest of them had been quick enough to do the same.

He discovered Bo and his mother inside one of the tents. Other rabbits were lying on the rooftops and on the shoreline. Using his strength, Uki carried them all, two at a time, and laid them out around the smouldering bonfire. He fetched blankets from the huts and tents and folded them into pillows. He brought water from the longhouse in a bucket and began to try and feed it to them, a drop at a time from a cloth. There were fifty-seven Gurdles – men, women and children alike – now stretched out over every plank of the platform outside the longhouse. After combing the banks and the trees around the village, he thought he had found everyone.

One of the huts he had visited looked like it belonged to a witch or doctor. There had been herbs and dried roots hanging from the ceiling. Clay jars and bowls of this and that on the shelves. *Perhaps I could find a cure?* he had thought, desperate to do something more to help. *Perhaps I could make them better?*

You're more likely to poison them, his dark voice had said. **You don't know dandelions from deadly nightshade.**

And it was true. There was absolutely nothing

he could do except watch and pray that they would recover.

Except they didn't.

What had started off as poison bites had become something much, much worse.

As the sun rose, Uki began to realise that the swarm of bugs had just been carriers for the *real* attack. Charice had filled them with one of her plagues. Even as Uki's body had healed itself, those of his friends had begun to stew with disease. The places they had been bitten began to drip black blood and sour-smelling orange pus. Their faint breath began to rattle in their lungs as they gasped and fought to stay alive.

Some of them began to murmur and mumble, saying strange, feverish things. When Uki put his paw to their heads, he could feel them burning up.

He tore blankets into strips and soaked them in the cold water of the lake, before placing them on the rabbits' foreheads. Anything to cool them down, to make them more comfortable. Again, it seemed useless.

In between tending to his patients, he had found

a broom and begun to sweep the village clear of the swathes of dead bugs. Perhaps they might still carry some infection. Perhaps it might help a little.

It was like sweeping piles of dead leaves. They rustled and crunched as he pushed them with his broom. Keeping a safe distance, he could still see how they had been warped and altered by Charice. There were dragonflies with eight eyes and cruel, curved jaws. There were stag beetles with swollen, bloated bodies that burst as he swept them. Smaller insects filled the gaps in between them like dust. Mosquitoes and midges, bluebottles and blowflies. Their bodies fell into the lake and drifted downstream in island-shaped clusters, like poisonous, evil lily pads.

It was noon when he heard the voice.

From somewhere on the bank, behind the shielding willow trees, a rabbit was calling.

'Hallooo! Hallooo! Is anybody there?'

Uki picked his way through the mass of sick rabbits, then scampered along the wooden walkway to the edge of the village. He got there just as the visiting rabbit pushed his way through the hanging willows on to the bank. It was a young male, dressed in Gurdle frogskin, carrying a bundle over his shoulder, tied to the end of his walking stave.

'Stop!' Uki shouted. 'Don't come into the village!'

The rabbit froze on the bank, staring at Uki in surprise. His eyes moved over the clustered boats, across the bank and up into the branches. Clearly he was wondering where all the sentries and guards had gone.

'What be goin' on, then?' he said. 'Where is everybody?'

Uki wondered how he could possibly explain what had happened and make the rabbit believe him. But he had to say something. If that rabbit set paw inside the village, he could fall sick, just like the others.

'There's been an attack,' he said. 'It was the Maggitches. Everyone in the village is sick with some kind of plague. You have to keep away!'

'Sick? Everyone?' The rabbit frowned at Uki, obviously wondering who this strange child was and whether he should believe him.

'Yes. Granny Maggitch and some others came

last night while the feast was going on. They put a kind of poison in the fire and now every single Gurdle is ill.' Uki left out the part about the swarm of flies. There was no way he could explain that without revealing the story of the spirits, and for all he knew this rabbit might be as unbelieving as Ma Gurdle.

'Gollop curse those Maggitches!' The rabbit threw his pack to the floor and stamped his foot. 'Are you sure it's a plague? My aunt and cousins are in there ...'

'I'm sure,' said Uki. 'I'm trying to look after them all, but you can't come in! You might catch it too and ... and I don't think any of them is going to survive.'

At that, the rabbit gasped. He put his paws to his head and paced up and down the bank. Uki had a good idea how he was feeling – desperate to do something, but completely unable to think what.

After a few moments, when the helplessness had finally sunk in, he turned back to Uki. 'I don't understand any of this,' he said. 'Who are you, and why are you still here if there's plague? How be it that you're not sick?'

'I was here with my friends and Charcoal,' said

Uki, trying to think of a convincing explanation. 'We helped a rabbit called Bo and he brought us here for the feast. My friends are ill too, and I think I might be coming down with it.' He did a little cough and tried to look unwell.

The rabbit took a step back. 'Will you . . . will you stay with them? Until the end, like?'

Uki nodded. 'There's not much I can do, but . . .'

'Bandylegs bless you,' said the rabbit. He reached down for the pack he had been carrying and threw it across the water to where Uki stood. 'There's some food and wine in there. I was bringing it to my aunt. If you need anything else, I can fetch it.'

'Thank you,' Uki said, pulling the pack firmly on to the boat. 'I think you'd better stay clear, though. Perhaps you should leave the Fenlands completely. Go somewhere far away.' *Because this plague will spread*, he added silently. *There's only a tiny chance I can stop Charice on my own, and if I fail, her diseases will be everywhere.*

'Maybe I will,' said the rabbit. 'I've got a wife and three nippers back in Reedwic. Otherwise I'd stay and help . . .'

'It's all right,' said Uki.

The rabbit turned to go and then paused, as if he had remembered something. 'Say,' he said. 'Were you travelling with two others? One of them with painted fur, on a giant hoppy thing?'

'A jerboa. Yes.'

'Then there's folk looking for you, back in town. Asking questions in the inns and whatnot. Questions about three children. Not very nice folk either.'

Uki felt his fur prickle as he realised who it could be. 'Is it an old woman? With a headscarf?'

'That be the one,' said the rabbit. 'And she has some shady sneakers with her. All becloaked and shifty. Then there's another too. A young chap with grey fur and fine armour. With a sword of real sky metal on his hip.'

Uki had an idea about who that was as well. 'Does he have a flask on his belt? Made of bone, with a silver cap?'

'Aye, that be correct. Old Pennyfeather said he was a Dusker. From a clan up north in the Coldwood.' The rabbit peered at Uki again, his head cocked on one side. 'What's a young nipper like you done to have that lot after you?'

Uki shrugged. Perhaps Jori could have come up with an explanation, but his mind had gone utterly blank. 'I'm just . . . just popular, I suppose?'

The rabbit nodded, tapping a finger to his nose. 'None of my beeswax. I understand. I won't say nothing to nobody, don't worry. I owe you that much for what you're doing. And there's no way they'll find you here.'

'Thank you,' said Uki.

'No, thank *you*,' said the rabbit. 'Thank you for seeing to my family. I'll . . . I'll make sure them Maggitches pay for this. Somehow.'

Uki wanted to tell him not to try, not to keep the old battles grinding on even longer, but he had already turned away and ducked under the willow branches. There had been tears in the rabbit's eyes as he left, knowing he would never see his family again.

And there were tears in Uki's too as he picked up the pack and headed back to the village square feeling more alone and helpless than ever.

*

There were parcels of biscuits and bread inside the pack, as well as some clay bottles of elderberry wine. Uki mixed some of the wine with water and did another round of his patients. They seemed to take the mixture a bit better than before. Perhaps the wine might give them some strength. Perhaps.

He found it was easier if he tried to keep busy. Every time he stopped to watch his friends, a surge of panic built up and threatened to overtake him. How could he go on without them? How could he possibly capture the last two spirits on his own?

He set about replacing all the damp cloths on the rabbits' foreheads, then trying them with more wine and water. By the time he'd finished that, the sky above was beginning to be tinged pink. A whole day had gone and there was no sign of anyone recovering.

Uki was thinking about lighting the bonfire again, to keep everyone warm through the oncoming night, when he noticed Kree stirring beneath her blanket. He rushed over to her side.

'Kree? Can you hear me? Are you feeling better?'

The little rabbit squinted at him through swollen

eyelids. She moved her mouth a fraction, and Uki wet it with some water from his cloth.

'Cold,' she said, her voice hardly more than a croak. 'Everything is cold.'

'I'm just about to light a fire,' said Uki. 'A big bonfire. It'll warm you up nicely, I promise!'

'Uki? Is that you?' Kree blinked again and tried to move her head. Uki knelt closer and took one of her blistered paws in his.

'Yes, it's me. I'm here.' A tear trickled down his nose and dripped on to Kree's blanket. 'Tell me what I can do to make you feel better. Tell me how to help you.'

'Mooka. How is Mooka?'

Uki looked round to where her jerboa lay, his side moving with shallow breaths. How could he tell her that the poor creature was close to dying? Would it be wrong to lie? 'He's fine,' Uki said eventually. 'I found him a bit of pasture to hop around in. He's nibbling the grass and ... and ... he misses you.'

Kree closed her other paw over his and gave it a weak squeeze. 'You're a bad liar, Uki. At least he will be with me on the Sky Plains. We will ride together again.'

'No!' Uki felt like shaking her, squeezing her, but he didn't dare move her wounded body too much. 'Don't say that! You're not going to die! You're not!'

'I think I am.' Kree's voice was just a whisper now, her eyes were closed again. 'I think it will be soon. Will you do something for me, Uki?'

Pawing away the tears that spilled from his eyes, Uki nodded. He found he couldn't speak. The words wouldn't come.

'Go back to the plains, once you're done. Find my parents and tell them I was sorry. They didn't really throw me out, you see. We had a big fight. My father wanted to use Mooka for leather to make a new tent. He said a tailless jerboa was useless. We fought about it so many times. One day he told me to get out and never come back.

'I don't think he meant it. He was just angry. I have a way of making people very angry, you know. I don't expect you've noticed, but it's true.

'I was angry too, so I left. I took Mooka and ran away. I've often thought . . . if I went back . . . if I said

171

sorry, I'm sure he would forgive me. He'd change his mind about Mooka too, if he could see how fast he is, how well I ride him . . .'

'He would,' whispered Uki. 'I know he would.'

'*Papa.*' Kree was looking up at the sky now. Uki wasn't even sure if she knew he was there. '*Uk noo ha, Papa.*'

She fell asleep again then, or passed out. Uki couldn't rouse her, not by gentle shaking, not by dripping water on her forehead. He had a horrid, pounding feeling that she might not ever speak again.

'I don't think she's long for this world. I don't think any of us are.' A broken voice came from beside him. It took Uki a moment to recognise it as Coal's. Leaving Kree to sleep, he hopped over to the smith's side.

'Are you expecting me to say sorry for all the bad things I've done in my life?' Coal tried to laugh, but all that came out was a dry croak. 'I don't think I'd get through the list.'

'You must be feeling better, though,' said Uki. 'You're awake. You're talking.'

Coal groaned. 'The fever's stopped. I just feel cold

now. Everything hurts. But don't get your hopes up. I've seen this in sicknesses. A moment of clarity before ...'

'Please,' said Uki, beginning to cry again. 'Don't say it. Don't go. I can't finish the job on my own.'

'Just do your best.' Coal's voice began to fade. 'You're strong enough.'

Uki shook his head. All his strength wouldn't be enough to face this. Not on his own.

'Uki.' Coal pulled at the collar of his tunic, dragging out a small golden locket on a chain. 'Do something for me?'

Uki nodded.

'When I'm ... gone ... into the Land Beyond. Will you bury me? Bury me with my locket.'

'Of course,' Uki said, forcing the words out. 'Is that ... your wife?'

'A lock of her fur,' said Coal, his eyes drifting closed. 'The last piece ... of my old life. Before my accident. I want to take it with me, when I go. You won't burn me, will you? I've been burnt enough ...'

'I won't,' said Uki. 'I promise.' But Coal had slipped back under. His chest still moved with his breathing, but it was weaker now. Hardly there ...

Expecting Jori to wake next, Uki moved to sit beside her. Half of him yearned for the chance to speak to her again, half dreaded not knowing what to say.

Either way, he didn't have to wait long. She began to murmur and then fought to open her eyes.

'Jori, it's me. It's Uki.' He pressed a piece of wet blanket to her head and dabbed at her eyes so she could open them. Between the swollen red eyelids, he saw a sliver of grey.

'Uki? Did we do it? Did we catch her?'

'Not yet.' Uki cursed himself again. 'Not quite. She got away, but as soon as you're better, we'll be after her again.'

'Not me. I don't think . . . I don't think I'm going anywhere.' She gave a long, violent shudder. Uki took off his cloak and spread it over her.

'Please, Jori,' he said. 'Don't leave me. I'm so sorry . . . This is all my fault.'

Jori stretched a paw out of the blankets and laid it on Uki's shoulder. The effort seemed to take all of her strength. 'No. Not your fault,' she whispered. 'I'm glad. Glad I met you. You're my best . . . best friend.'

Her paw fell away, and she let out a pained, gasping breath. At her nose, a fat droplet of bright red blood formed and then trickled down the side of her face.

Uki sat and looked at it. That splash of vivid red against the grey fur. The life of his friend was in that drop, he thought, all her thoughts and hopes and scowls and laughs ... everything that made up Jori.

And now it had just trickled away.

CHAPTER TEN

Lord Maggety-Pie

For many long, heartbroken minutes, Uki sat and stared at the streak of blood on his friend's face. It was somehow worse than seeing the scores of seeping bites all over her body. Worse than hearing her breath rattle or feeling her paw drop, lifeless, away from his shoulder.

He was still staring when two magpies flew overhead, breaking the silence with their stuttering, cackling cries. *Ak-ak-ak-akkak-ak!*

Uki stopped his mourning, watching them flutter past, remembering the moment outside the mayor's fortress in Syn when all had seemed hopeless. He had seen two magpies then, when he'd thought about the rope. They had shown him he was on the right track, as if they were some kind of sign or message.

But what could they be telling him now? What had he been doing when they appeared?

Nothing. Just staring at Jori's blood and feeling hollow, alone and empty.

Blood.

It came to him, then.

He was the only rabbit not to be sick. Because of Iffrit. Because of how the spirit had merged with him. But the poison from the insects had gone into him, just the same. His body had been filled with it – he had even felt it. So what had killed it off? How had it been burned away?

'Iffrit is in my *blood.*' He spoke the words aloud, even though there was no rabbit left awake to hear them.

Uki jumped up, holding his paws out in front of him. *Did that mean . . . ? Could it be possible?* What if he gave some of his blood to Jori and the others? Would it contain enough of Iffrit to kill Charice's plague? Could there be tiny pieces of the fire guardian in it that would fight off the infection somehow?

He had to try.

Careful not to move her too much, he pulled back the blankets from Jori and drew her sword. The evening sun gleamed along the blade, picking out the ripples in the steel. He had expected it to be heavy – and it did seem to have a great, solid weight – but it was so well balanced, it sat perfectly in his paw.

'Don't chop off a finger, Uki,' he muttered to himself as he touched the tip. Wincing, he pushed very gently. There was a sharp, burning feeling as the edge sliced straight through his fur and into his flesh.

'Ow!'

He held up his finger and saw blood welling there. Quite a lot, actually. The sword was *very* sharp. Setting it down, he moved back to Jori and dangled his bleeding finger near her open mouth. A drop fell on to her tongue and trickled back into her throat. He saw her neck move in reflex. She had swallowed it.

Please work, please work, he prayed to himself,

moving on to do the same for Kree and Coal before his rapid-healing power stitched his wound shut. He even braved the long, curved teeth of Mooka to smear some on the jerboa's tongue.

A little while had passed by the time he got back to Jori. He stood, watching her, holding his breath. If this didn't work, there was nothing else he could try. And he was certain she wouldn't live to see the morning.

One minute crawled by, then another. The last dregs of hope were just beginning to drain out of him when he noticed something: a flicker beneath Jori's eyelids.

Could it be? He moved closer, willing it to happen again. 'Come on, Jori,' he said, under his breath. 'Come *on*.'

Her eyes flickered again. A trembling, butterfly flutter.

Uki took her hand. Did it feel warmer, or was it his imagination?

And then she coughed.

'Yes!' Uki punched the air. The blood was working!

He watched for a few moments more. Jori was

still fast asleep, but she moved and twitched like a normal sleeper now, not the stony, cold sleep of the dying she had been lost in. She smacked her lips and groaned a little. Her ears gave a twitch.

Looking across, Uki saw Coal and Kree had begun to stir as well. They might take some time to come back to themselves, but the process had begun.

Relief spread over Uki like the sun breaking through storm clouds. Death had been so close, he was surprised he hadn't seen Nixha herself, stalking through the village with her bow.

Seeing as nobody was watching him, Uki did a little dance right there on the raft. He hopped and jigged and skipped, until he had spun himself around to face all the other rabbits, still in the grip of plague.

Oh, he thought. *That's going to take a* lot *of blood.*

*

By the time he had finished, it was dark. He had needed to jab the tips of all his fingers as he went around the fifty-seven Gurdles, dabbing a drop of blood into each of their mouths. The tiny cuts had healed quickly, thanks to Iffrit's powers, but all that spiking and squeezing had made him feel a bit queasy.

He had just kindled a fire on the bronze stand and was feeding it some logs, when he heard his name being called. Faintly at first, but growing stronger.

He turned around to see Jori, sitting up amongst her blankets. She still looked terrible – her face all bloated with bites and stings – but her eyes were open.

'Uki?' Her voice was weak and crackling with dryness. 'Is that you?'

He threw a few logs into the growing blaze and dashed over to his friend, throwing his arms around her and squeezing until she yelped.

'Ow! Stop! Everything hurts . . .'

'Sorry! Sorry!' Uki let her go and then ran to grab the water pail. He scooped out a cupful and held it to her lips. 'Here, drink this,' he said. 'You've been very ill. I thought you were going to die!'

Jori took a gulp from the cup and then two or three more. When it was empty, she sat back and groaned. 'Was it those bugs?' she said. 'I remember them hitting us. They were biting me all over . . .'

'Yes,' said Uki. 'They were carrying some kind of plague. Everyone in the village had it, but I recovered. I didn't know what to do, until I thought of giving you all some of my blood.'

'Blood?' Even under the scores of bites and blisters, Jori looked horrified.

'Just a drop,' said Uki. 'I guessed it might have something in it from Iffrit. Something that could fight off Charice's sickness.'

'Of course. Iffrit must have been immune to all her diseases. Otherwise she could just have poisoned him and escaped. That was good thinking.'

'Thank you,' said Uki. 'I'm hoping all the others will wake up soon too.'

'Then you'd better get some food on,' said Jori. 'I can't move a whisker without it hurting, but I'm as hungry as a starved badger.'

*

Uki didn't know much about cooking, but he had watched his mother make soup many times. He found a tripod big enough to hold a large pot and set it up over the fire. Then, using a candle to light his way, he raided all the nearby houses for vegetables. Turnips, onions, potatoes, carrots; he threw them into the pot with some water and let it boil and boil.

When the vegetables were soft, he mashed them up until he was left with a mushy puree. It probably didn't taste too good, but he figured the poorly rabbits wouldn't care.

By the time he'd finished, nearly all of them were awake, groaning in pain and staring around with bloodshot, bleary eyes.

He paused in his cooking to hug Kree and pat Coal awkwardly on the shoulder. He even gave Mooka a cuddle and was rewarded with a *neek*. The jerboa seemed to understand that Uki had saved him.

Then he scooped a bowl of soup from the pot and began to offer it to them, holding the spoon like a father with his baby, patiently waiting as they slurped up tiny mouthfuls. He mopped their chins, gave them some water, then settled them in their blankets again, the sound of their gentle, painless breathing like music to his ears.

Once his friends had eaten, he did the rounds once more, tending to every rabbit, spoon-feeding each one. He told them what had happened, assured them all their loved ones were safe, and made them as comfortable as he could. At some point during the night, after all his patients had woken, eaten and fallen asleep again, Uki collapsed amongst them, every bone aching from exhaustion, and slept himself.

*

It took three whole days for the Gurdles to recover. The lumps and swellings from the bites gradually went down. Eyes opened, rabbits started hobbling around and then walking. By the end of the third day, they had all gone back to their boats, and the square in front of Ma Gurdle's longhouse was empty.

All that time, Uki had worried about Charice. He knew she would be gathering her strength, building up a new cloud of plague-bearing bugs. How long before she had enough to attack Reedwic? Or to spread her diseases outside of the Fenlands to other warrens?

Just as the sun was setting on the third day, Ma Gurdle summoned Uki and the others to her house. They had been staying at Bo's boat-tent, sleeping on the floor, with Mooka tied up outside on deck. Jori, Kree and Coal were almost back to full health now, although they still had speckles of crusted blood here and there where the insects had bitten them. You could see them the most on Coal, on the patches of bare skin and his ears. It looked like he'd been attacked by a giant hedgehog, or rolled back and forth in a bed of pins.

They stood together inside Ma's house, waiting for her to hobble out from her bedchamber. The sickness had hit her hard and she was having trouble walking. Her fur was flecked with scabs as well, and her giant frog still hadn't returned.

Two other Gurdles helped her to her chair, where she sat, huddled in her feather cloak, staring hard at Uki and his friends. There was a look of cold, calculating fury in her eyes and Uki worried it might be for him, even though he had just saved her life.

'You's probably wondering why I asked you here,' she said.

'We haven't . . . done anything wrong, have we?' Uki asked.

'Wrong?' Ma Gurdle opened her mouth and let out a long wheeze that might have been a laugh. 'Bless my bunions, no. If it wasn't for you, Uki, we'd all be feeding the eels right now. The whole Gurdle clan. Every member of my family. No, nothing you could ever do would be wrong by us. Not for as long as you lived.'

Uki blushed under his fur. Everywhere he went in the village, rabbits were thanking him and hugging him. All the attention and gratitude was so new, so strange to Uki. To have the love of a whole village, when all he had known from his own was hatred. Was this what being part of a tribe was supposed to be like? Rabbits actually pleased to see him, instead of running in fear? Kind words instead of insults? How he wished his mother could be here to see him being treated like a friend instead of an outcast.

He even had a pile of gifts back at Bo's house. Mostly pairs of frogskin trousers and necklaces of snakes' fangs. And all just for using the powers that had come to him almost by accident. He really didn't feel as though he deserved such special treatment.

'I called you here,' Ma Gurdle continued, 'because you asked me something, back before them thrice-damned Maggitches set their bugs on us. You asked for our help to find them, so you could stop them stinking up the fen with their poison curse.'

'Yes,' said Uki. 'Now I know that Granny Maggitch is behind all the sick marsh creatures. I have to stop her before she attacks anybody else.'

'Last time, I said no to you, I recall.'

Uki nodded. It seemed like months ago, instead of just a few days.

'Well, I won't be making that mistake again.' Ma Gurdle reached out for Uki's paw and held it tight. 'We Gurdles are with you, Lord Maggety-Pie. Any help you need, we'll give it. It's high time we took care of them Maggitches once and for all. We'll take you right to them and then we can box their bollycrackers together. What d'you say to that?'

'That ... that would be amazing!' Uki said.

'Righto, then.' Ma Gurdle let go of his paw and stood up, with help from the rabbits standing by her chair. 'We'll need to send out a scout or two first. I reckon they's squirrelled themselves away on Gollop's Mound, but we ought to be sure. Then the whole family will head out together. There's going to be a reckoning. A muckle gurt reckoning.'

'Thank you,' said Uki, as Ma Gurdle was helped back to her bedchamber. 'Thank you very much!'

Ma Gurdle waved a hand as she disappeared through a door at the back of the house. Coal gave a low whistle. 'A reckoning, eh? I've heard them talk about those. The last one was fifty years ago or more.'

'What are they?' Kree asked. 'Some kind of fight? Or maybe a racing challenge, like the plains tribes have?'

'More like a war,' said Coal. 'One that might settle the feud between the families once and for all.'

'Perhaps we should go with the scouts tomorrow,' said Uki. 'If we can find the Maggitches and sneak into their camp, there might not have to be any fighting. I only want to stop Charice. I don't want anyone to be hurt.'

'Good idea, Uki,' said Jori. 'Or should I say ... *Lord Maggety-Pie.*'

'Please don't,' said Uki. 'I don't ever want to be called that again.'

'I've just made up a song,' said Kree. *'Maggety-Pie, Maggety-Pie, kissed a frog and made it cry!'*

And, as Uki winced and blushed some more, she sang it over and over, all the way back to Bo's house.

CHAPTER ELEVEN

Glopstickers

The Gurdles were happy enough for Uki and Jori to join them on their scouting trip. Kree had decided to stay in the village with Mooka. Most of the expedition was going to be by boat and she didn't think the jerboa would cope very well, not after the stress of being so ill.

There were three rabbits going with them. Ma Gurdle had volunteered some of her best scouts. Hitch and Yurdle were two of her sons and Rawnie was the tribe's finest hunter. She had more snake fangs on her necklace than anyone.

The boat they took was called the *Sleek Hawker*. It was a flat-bottomed dinghy, with a stubby mast and a muddy-green sail which was currently rigged up as a tent-like canopy, with Rawnie's bedroll and blankets beneath. As Uki and Jori watched, the Gurdle hunter hopped aboard her craft and dashed about, untying knots and coiling ropes. Within a few minutes, she had the sail wrapped around the boom arm that jutted from the mast. All her bedding, pots and pans were stowed out of sight, and two oars had appeared in the rowlocks. She also brought out a long pole, which she passed up to Hitch.

'Ready to cast off,' she said, hopping up to the prow. 'Yurdle will row, Hitch will steer, unless we get weedbound. Then he can punt us free. You two mollygogglers can sit in the stern.'

Coal was standing with them. Uki thought he might have liked to come, but there was no room in the boat. 'Be careful, you two,' he said. 'You're just going out to find where the Maggitches are. Stay in the boat and keep quiet.'

'We can take care of ourselves, thank you,' Jori replied, stepping briskly into the dinghy. Uki paused to give Coal a smile, hoping to make up for his friend's bluntness.

'We'll be fine,' he said. 'Look after Kree and Mooka for us.'

'Will do.' Coal held out his hammer to help Uki into the boat. It rocked and swayed as he stepped in, but after spending a few days on the floating Gurdle village, he found his legs were used to it.

'Casting off,' said Hitch. He untied the ropes that joined the *Sleek Hawker* to the rest of the houses, then gave it a shove with his pole. As it drifted out into the lake, he leaped from the platform, landing in the stern and making the boat bob alarmingly. Uki yelped and clung on to the sides.

'Show-off,' said Yurdle, grinning back at his brother. He took the oars and began to row – deep strokes that drove the boat swishing through the water. Hitch sat at the tiller, his pole resting on his knees, and steered them across the lake.

'Will we have to go far?' Jori asked. She seemed to be clutching the sides as tightly as Uki. *Perhaps*, he thought, *for all her experience of the world, she hasn't spent a lot of time in boats.*

'That be depending,' said Rawnie. 'Ma reckons them Maggitches has dug in on Gollop's Mound. Won't take us too long to get there. If'n they're somewhere else ... we could be out all day. Maybe longer.'

Uki looked at the dark water rippling by on either side of him. There was nothing between it and his feet but a thin layer of wood. He gripped his seat even harder and tried to stop his ears from trembling.

They rowed out of the lake, drifting underneath the trailing branches of the willows, which reached down to tickle their noses and leave a shower of catkins all over them. The *Sleek Hawker* emerged on to a winding river, high walls of bulrushes and reeds on either side.

Rawnie climbed up on to the prow, leaning out over the water with a long, bronze-tipped spear in her paws. Her head twitched to and fro as she stared at the reeds and the surface of the water, searching, searching for something.

'Erm ... what are you looking for?' Uki asked, almost dreading to hear the answer.

'Snakes,' she replied. Uki winced.

'We're going right into zaggert grounds now,' said Yurdle, as he strained at the oars. 'Vipers, you mudwalkers call 'em. Adders. Big, venomous snakes.'

'Exactly how big?' Jori asked. Her paw moved to rest on her sword hilt.

'Depends,' said Hitch. 'They start off the size of one of you nippers. Then they just keeps on growing. I've heard tell of ones bigger than an oak tree, out by Toadtwitch Lake.'

The two brothers sniggered a little, so Uki didn't know whether they were joking or not. But when Rawnie spoke, her voice was deadly serious.

'Fully grown zaggerts are big,' she said. 'Big enough to eat one of us whole. They swim too, but they don't usually strike in the water. It's when we go on land that we'll have to be careful. Especially if we's near the reeds. They hide in them and then shoots out – whip-quick – so fast there's nothing you can do about it.'

'But you hunt them, don't you?' Uki said. 'You're good at killing them?'

'Younglings, mostly. One or two gurters. If I see one big enough to eat me, I run.' Rawnie took her eyes off the water long enough to spare Uki a glance. A hard, serious look that made his fur stand on end. Uki took a spear from his harness and began to stare at the passing reeds as well.

They rowed for an hour or so, with Hitch having to stand and punt every now and then, when Yurdle's oars became tangled in weed. Tall reeds hemmed them in, their bearded heads nodding in time to the wind. There was birdsong everywhere – coots hooting, ducks quacking. Dragonflies darted about, their wings shining like shards of floating glass.

Thankfully, the only wildlife they saw was small. Finches, geese, moorhens and herons. A flash of blue and orange that Hitch said was a kingfisher, diving into the river to catch her supper.

Uki looked out for signs of Charice's plague amongst the creatures. Here and there a dead fish floated, its pale belly marked with angry red sores. They seemed to see more of them as they moved further away from Gurdle territory, as they edged closer to the ancient spirit that Uki could feel pulsing in the back of his head.

When the river began to open out, Hitch steered

the boat over to the bank. Rawnie leaped ashore, tying the painter to a tree root and holding the boat steady for the rest to disembark.

'Downriver is Blacksand Bay,' she said. 'A nice little cove for sea craft to land in. We smuggle the booty up the river here, and the Spikers don't know a thing about it.'

'Can't we get to Gollop's Mound by sailing?' Uki asked. Even though it was just a few planks of wood, he felt safer inside the *Sleek Hawker* than he did walking past the reed beds on foot. Every step, waiting for a snake's head to come shooting out and bite him. His reactions were fast, true, but he doubted they were quicker than a striking viper. And even Iffrit's healing wouldn't work very well from inside an adder's stomach.

'No streams or rivers go that way,' said Hitch. 'We can take this path for a bit, then we have to glopstalk.'

'Glopstalk?'

'Walk through the mud, like. In the marsh.'

Uki and Jori looked at each other. It was hard to say who was the most horrified.

The riverbank they stepped on to was high, dry land with thick trees and bushes on the other side of the reeds. A well-worn path led alongside the river and they followed it back the way they had rowed a little, before Rawnie stopped by a gap in the hedgerow. She pointed through it, southwards, to where the view opened up. Uki saw an expanse of fen: patches of meadow grass, dotted here and there with pools and clusters of reeds. Further off, the pools seemed to join together, making a wide strip of brown mud. In the distance was a high, round hill, covered with bushes and the spindly fingers of dead trees.

'Gollop's Mound,' Rawnie said.

As soon as Uki saw it, he felt a pulsing pain in his head. Charice was there, he was sure of it. And something else too. Another spirit? The waves of queasiness that seemed to flow from the place blurred his senses. He couldn't be sure.

'Well,' said Jori. 'We've seen it. Perhaps we should head back now?'

'Not yet, mudwalker,' said Rawnie. 'We need to get a bit nearer. Close enough to see if them Maggitches is there.'

Twirling her spear, Rawnie hopped down from the bank and began to follow a faint path across the meadow. Hitch and Yurdle followed, and there was nothing Uki and Jori could do except join them.

The sun was nearly at its noon point in the sky when they saw the snake.

They had picked their way around most of the marshy pools and were heading across the last piece of dry grassland when Rawnie suddenly stopped, dropping to a crouch and spreading both arms wide in warning.

'Everybody halt!' she hissed. 'Don't take another step!'

Uki froze in mid-stride, one foot still off the ground. He held his breath, fighting for balance, eyes darting everywhere. Where was the danger?

Then he saw it. From a patch of reeds off to their left, what he'd thought was a mound of earth began to twitch, before lazily uncoiling. Metre after metre of black and brown scaled skin unspooling into the twisting form of a serpent at least five times as long as he was.

It had a broad, paddle-shaped head and two

round eyes with a sinister red tinge. Tongue flicking, it moved from side to side as it slithered through the grass in front of them. As it flowed across the ground, Uki could see the black markings made a zigzag pattern along its back. The same markings he had seen on the Maggitches' snakeskin cloaks.

'Don't wiggle a whisker,' whispered Rawnie. 'It can sense vibrations through the ground.'

Uki's balance was failing, but he dared not set his foot down in case the bump of paw on earth drew the snake's attention. He flailed his arms a little, trying to keep upright. He hadn't even let out his breath. His chest felt like it was going to burst.

Finally, thank the Goddess, the adder reached a wide pool of muddy brown water and slid inside. It swam off, body wriggling, head held clear, leaving Uki and the others in peace.

'By all the numbers!' Jori let out the breath she had been holding, just like Uki. He gasped and set his foot down – gently, in case the snake still felt it from wherever it had swum to.

'I don't think we were in any danger,' said

Rawnie. 'Did you see its fat stomach? It had eaten something not long ago.'

Uki had indeed noticed a bulge halfway down the snake's body. It had looked about the same size as an adult rabbit.

'Was the snake healthy?' he asked. 'I mean, do you think it had any of the Maggitch plagues?'

'Hard to tell from this distance,' said Rawnie. 'We can follow it if you like? Try and get a better look?'

'No!' Uki answered so quickly, it made the snake-hunter blink. 'I was just wondering. Forget I said anything. Please.'

'Plague-carrying snakes,' Jori muttered. 'That's all we need.'

'You mudwalkers will be pleased to know it's not far now,' said Hitch, as the others stared after the adder. 'We'll just get close enough to check for firesmoke. Maybe spot some movement on the hill. We can watch from that copse over there.'

He pointed to a stand of trees poking out from the swampy mud. Praying that there were no more adders about, they made their way to the edge of the grassland and began to wade.

*

The swamp didn't grab them immediately. It crept up, slow and hungry.

First, Uki's galoshed paws started to squelch. Water was bubbling up through the grass with each step, and he sank a little deeper every time he moved.

Soon, he was up to his ankles. The grass had petered out, replaced with scratchy, straggly reeds. In between the clumps were pools of muddy brown water. When he looked closely, Uki could see twitching things swimming quickly out of his path.

Another few metres, and the water was up past his knees. It was so dark and brothy, he couldn't see what he was standing in, but he could feel the *suck-schlop* of mud and slime every time he pulled a paw free. He kept close behind Hitch and Rawnie, both of whom were prodding ahead of them with spear and pole, making sure they didn't step into a sinkhole or patch of quickmud.

'Isn't there ... some kind of path?' Jori asked, fighting to pull her leg free.

'This *is* a path, you big wazzock,' said Rawnie, over her shoulder. Uki cringed. It really wasn't a good idea to call a trained assassin names. He could hear Jori muttering something about 'marsh-grubbing halfwits', and could picture the scowl on her face without even looking.

It certainly wasn't like any kind of path Uki had ever seen. Although Rawnie *did* seem to know where she was going, winding around patches of water that looked deeper than the others, gradually – oh, so gradually – inching closer to the copse of trees they were going to spy from.

You should have stayed back in the village, his dark voice muttered in his ear. **There was no need for you to be here. Now you're going to get sucked under the mud, or eaten by a snake. Maybe both.**

There might still be a chance, Uki told himself. *A chance I could slip away from Rawnie and get into the Maggitch camp. I could capture Charice before there has to be any fighting.*

Slip away? Sneak up *there?*

Uki looked across the marsh between him and Gollop's Mound. Even if he could get away from the others, he was moving at the pace of a one-legged badger, stuck in a barrel of treacle. They would be able to hear the *schlop, schlop* of his slow footsteps from miles away. And that's if he didn't fall down an underwater hole first.

'Whose stupid idea was this?' Jori said, drawing level with him.

'I think it might have been mine. Sorry.'

'Let's just get it over with and get back to the village,' said Jori. 'The quicker we're out of these fens, the better.'

A worrying thought occurred to Uki. If it was this tricky to get to the mound, how were the Gurdles planning to mount their great attack? He caught up with Rawnie and asked her.

'We'll come at night,' she said. 'We know the paths well enough. By sun-up, we'll all be at the bottom of the mound, if that's where them Maggitches is hiding. Then we just have to run up it and give them a good paddlewhacking.'

Uki was about to suggest that it might not be as easy as all that, when something slithered through the mud in front of him. Something big and wriggly. He let out a yelp.

'Just a hoppet,' said Rawnie, poking the mud with

her spear butt. A slimy, long-legged creature burst upwards with a *plop* and then began to squirm its way to the nearest pool. 'Only a small one too.'

It was the size of my head! Uki started to say, when he spotted a movement at the pool's edge. It had looked like a pair of eyes, ducking down under the water. There for an instant, then gone, any ripples it might have made disguised by those of the escaping frog.

'Did you see that?' he asked, but everyone's attention was fixed on the muddy water in front of them.

'Just keep moving,' said Rawnie. 'We'll soon be out of this glop.'

Uki carried on, step by slurping step. He kept a careful watch on the water, though, and a few minutes later saw the eyes again. This time it looked as if they had ears behind them. Long ones. *Rabbit* ones.

'There's something …' he began to say, when a paw shot out of the mud beside him and grabbed his leg.

'Glopstickers!' Hitch yelled, and then there were

suddenly explosions of water and muck all around as rabbits burst up from below the surface.

'Maggitch troops!' Rawnie shouted. 'They come from beneath the mud! Bunch together!'

Uki had a glimpse of several mud-coated figures, dressed in stitched snakeskin with some kind of masks and breathing tubes over their mouths. They had appeared from all directions, surrounding them completely. Jori had her sword drawn, the others were brandishing their spears.

'Jori,' he called, trying to move closer to her, but his leg was still gripped tight, right around his ankle. He strained, trying to use his strength to break free, but all the mud and water made it hard to get any traction.

Just as he felt his attacker's grip begin to slide, another pair of paws grabbed his foot, then more around his waist. Just how many of these Glopstickers were there?

Uki flailed, feeling his legs slipping out from under him. He went down on his side – cold, clammy mud flooding into his clothes, soaking through his fur. He tried to stand up again, but the paws were pulling, pulling him . . . backwards, downwards into the swamp.

Jori was screaming. 'Uki!'

He had one last glimpse of her, struggling towards him through the marsh, her paw outstretched, and then he was dragged down . . . gone . . . under the surface.

Slime, water, silt – it bubbled over his head, flooding his ears and nostrils. He could taste gritty, dank earth, feel slippery wetness squidging everywhere he tried to grip or stand. And always the paws of the Maggitch warriors, pulling him deeper, deeper into the muddy darkness . . .

CHAPTER TWELVE

The Pit

Uki woke with a start.

So cold . . . and . . . muddy?

Yes. Freezing, wet mud *everywhere* . . . and the fading edges of some dream where he was watching himself, huddled at the bottom of a pit.

He peeled his eyes open and sneezed globules of swamp slime from his blocked nose. His cloak, shirt and jerkin were heavy with mud and marsh water. They slapped against his fur when he moved.

His eyes adjusted to the gloomy light and he looked around . . . he *was* huddled in the bottom of a pit. One dug out of the mud, a good four metres deep. There was a circle of open sky above, covered by a grid of wooden poles, lashed together. It was dank, and stank of wet earth and rotten pondweed. The floor and the walls were slippery and soggy. Every time Uki moved, he could hear squelching. His paws slipped as he struggled to sit upright.

What had happened? He remembered walking through the marsh, trying to get to the trees. Then the paws had grabbed him, pulled him under . . .

Glopstickers. That's what Rawnie had called them. Maggitch warriors who had been hiding *under* the mud and water, masks and tubes allowing them to breathe. They had pulled him down with them, before Jori could get to him . . .

Jori! He peered around the pit, his eyes still stinging from the filthy swamp water. Was she here? Had they captured her too?

He thought he could make out a figure, propped against the wall opposite him. Slithering and sliding, he made his way across on paws and knees, as quickly as he could. His body seemed reluctant to respond. Where was his strength? His energy? But there was no time to worry about that.

'Jori?' He reached the slumped body, knuckling the dirt out of his eyes with his paws and blinking to see better. 'Jori, is that you?'

The rabbit didn't answer, and as Uki peered closer he could see why. It was dead. Long dead. The fur and flesh of its face had been eaten away to reveal bone. A skull face, with blank sockets for eyes and a row of grinning teeth.

Uki yelped and pedalled backwards, pushing himself away from the body. Out of reach of its skeletal grasp.

Don't be so stupid, his dark voice chided him. **It can't hurt you. Whoever it was has been dead for months.**

'Dead for months,' Uki repeated. 'Can't hurt me.'

As his breathing slowed, he looked closer at the unfortunate rabbit. Was it a Gurdle? Maybe a Shrike? No, the clothes were wrong. It wore faded woven trousers and shirt, with a neckerchief of tattered tartan cloth. No frogskin leather or crimson armour. Not even any boots. If anything, it was dressed like rabbits from the north. From Nether and the twin cities. So how had it come to be here, trapped in a Maggitch pit?

One of Nurg's poor brothers. Uki remembered the three rabbits that had been the first victims of the escaped spirits. Simple hunters from Nether, they had been used like pack rats, ferrying Valkus, Charice and Mortix across Hulstland to find better, more powerful hosts. Uki and his friends had found one of them, still alive, outside the walls of Nys. Perhaps this one had been made to walk all the way to the Fenlands. Perhaps the Maggitches had captured him, and then Charice had slipped out, preferring to control the body of Granny Maggitch herself.

'Sorry, Nurg's brother. If that is you,' Uki whispered. 'Sorry I didn't get here in time.'

Just staring at that blank, grinning face made Uki uncomfortable. He had to find a way out of this pit, before he too ended up having the flesh eaten off his bones by worms.

Leaning on the wall for support, he managed to get up. He still couldn't understand why he felt so weak. Was it another plague? One his powers couldn't fight off? Was it the cold, clinging mud?

He used his paws to try and scrape some of it from his clothes. And that was when he noticed it ...

His harness. It was gone.

Uki panicked.

His spears, harness, buckle, crystals ... the Maggitches must have taken them when he was unconscious. Before throwing him in the pit.

He still had the powers of Iffrit. They were entwined with every cell in his body, they couldn't be removed ... but the trapped spirits in the crystals ... the boosts to his strength and speed they had given him were gone. This weakness, the chill and aching – that was how it felt to be a normal rabbit again. Vulnerable, helpless. And with no way to trap Charice, even if he did get the chance.

I have to get out of here!

Uki turned to the wall and started to climb. Or rather, he flailed at the mud, clawing out soggy handfuls of clay, tumbling to the wet floor over and over again. He jumped, slid, scrambled, tumbled ... Soon he was caked from head to foot in even more brown slime and his every muscle burned from the exertion.

He knelt, resting his head against the wall and panting for breath.

Heh-heh-heeeech.

A sound came from behind him. A breathy kind of wheezing noise at the edge of his hearing. Uki froze, ears pricked, and heard it again.

There was someone else in the pit with him. And they were laughing.

He peered into the darkness at the furthest edge of the muddy hole. The daylight from above didn't reach there. In the shadows he could make out a bulbous shape, up against the wall. Was it a rabbit?

The laugh came again – little more than a wet, raspy cackle. The lumpy mass moved slightly, and Uki caught a glint of eyes peering out at him.

Tired, wary, he took a step closer. 'Hello? Who's there?'

He heard a groan, feverish, not unlike the sounds his recent patients had made in the village. The rattling laugh came again too. There was more than one rabbit.

Uki took another step. The longer he stared into the darkness, the more clearly he could see. The large shape was an enormous rabbit, wrapped in a muddy cloak. A smaller, spindlier creature was clutched in its arms. The big one seemed to be asleep, or unconscious at least, but the smaller one was watching Uki with cold, spiteful eyes.

'Fancy meeting you here,' it said, and then laughed again. Another hissing rattle that ended in a fit of coughing.

Necripha, Uki realised. *And the big rabbit must be Balto.*

He scooted back to the other side of the pit, as far as he could go, ready to run, jump ... anything he could to get away from them.

The last time he had come face to face with the pair, Balto had been about to cut him open. They had wanted Iffrit's power and were more than ready to kill him to get it.

What if they came for him now? There was no way out of this pit. With the boosted strength from the crystals he might have been able to beat them, but he alone was no match for Balto. Iffrit had given him many gifts, but they depended on having the trapped spirits nearby. Without them, all Uki's powers would slowly drain away. And if that went on long enough, he would fade and die with them. By rights, he should be dead anyway. It was only Iffrit's stitching that held him together.

Uki tensed his muscles, preparing to fight and run. Even if all he managed was to lead them on a chase round and round the bottom of this pit, he wasn't going to go easily. They would have to battle to take Iffrit from him . . .

Except they weren't even trying to stand up.

Uki pricked his ears, listening with his head cocked. He could hear a phlegmy gasping sound every time Balto breathed. There was a higher, reedy whistling too that must be Necripha's breath. And beneath the damp, slimy smell of the mud, he could detect a trace of sickness. The sour scent of feverish sweat that he recognised from when the Gurdles were gripped by plague.

They were ill.

Charice had infected them. They couldn't come after him because they were dying.

Thank the Goddess, Uki thought, allowing himself to relax. And then instantly felt bad for feeling such relief over another creature's suffering. He wondered how far along they were. How many days or hours they had left.

'Are you sick, little pest?' When Necripha spoke, her voice was broken and feeble. 'I can't tell under all that mud. Are your eyes swelling? Is your skin beginning to bubble and burst?'

Uki didn't speak, not for a long time. This was his enemy, his hunter. The creature who had been on his trail since he came back from the dead. When he had sensed another being, up on Gollop's Mound, it had been *her*.

But there was nothing Necripha could do to him now. She could barely even speak. As long as he kept his distance, she was harmless.

Just ignore her, he thought. *Soon she'll be too sick to talk. She'll be too sick to do anything.*

Stupid, his dark voice chipped in. **Just think of what she knows. She's as old as the spirits themselves. She must have secrets about them – weaknesses that you could use. If you**

don't try and prise them out of her, they'll be gone forever.

Secrets. Weaknesses.

Just *talking* to her wouldn't hurt, Uki supposed. As long as he was careful not to get tricked. As long as he remembered it was an evil spirit he was dealing with, not the old, dying rabbit that she appeared to be.

'I'm not sick,' he said, breaking the silence.

There was a rustling sound and a groan from Balto as Necripha moved to see Uki more clearly. 'Ah,' she said. 'I didn't think you would be. The fire guardian gave you *all* of his powers when he spliced himself with you, didn't he? Every last scrap. A complete and total bonding.'

'I suppose so,' said Uki. 'Iffrit was so weak at the time. He was fading.' He knew little of the magic the spirits could work, even though he was joined with one.

'I suspected as much when I first met you. How very noble of him. And how very annoying. Even if we had managed to crack you open, there would have been nothing of Iffrit left to take. And yet it was clever of him too. The four spirits might have managed to beat him together, but they will have no chance when they are trapped in separate prisons. If, by some miracle, you manage to get them all, that is.'

Uki needed to change the subject. To get Necripha talking about herself and how important she was. But he had to do it carefully, without her discovering what he was up to. How he wished Jori was here. What would she say in his place?

'How ... how did you end up in here?' he asked. 'I thought you were behind us.'

'Saw me in one of your visions, did you?' Necripha coughed and spat something gloopy into the mud. 'We *were* behind you. You'd left Reedwic by the time we got there. My stupid agent said you'd gone into the fen. He said you had a smith with you that worked for one of the savage tribes here. That he could find their village. Like a fool, I believed him.'

'The rabbit with the purple cloak. The one who sent the bat. Where is he now?'

'Inside a viper's belly. As are two others. Three more got sucked down, drowned in the mud. They were gone before Balto could pull them out.'

'And then the Maggitches found you?'

Necripha coughed again. Her voice seemed to be getting weaker. 'Yes. We were wandering ... lost. These masked rabbits burst up from under the water. Ingenious breathing tubes ... I didn't know they could do that. They brought us to their warren, on top of this hill. And that's where we saw Charice. But don't you know this? Haven't you been looking through my eyes?'

Uki shook his head. Come to think of it, he hadn't had any recent visions of Necripha, not until just moments ago when he saw himself, huddled in a sorry ball of mud.

'Strange. Maybe it's Charice's power. I've been feeling it ... pounding in my head for days. So difficult to think clearly.'

Uki had too, but he could sense Necripha turning the conversation round to him again. He wanted to find out what she knew about the spirits ...

'What did she do when she captured you? Charice, I mean?'

'Do? She threw us in this pit, that's what she did. After poisoning us ... with this plague. I tried to talk sense to her. To make her ... join me, but her brain has been warped. All the sickness and disease ... changed her. She's more lost now than ever before ...'

This is it, Uki thought. *She's talking about the past. Keep her going.*

'Wasn't she always like that, then? Back before the Ancients locked her away?'

'I don't think so. My memories of that time ... so hazy ... There must have been *something* wrong with her, for them to put her in that prison. She must have failed at what they created her for.'

Uki knew this was true, thanks to the memories he had gained from Iffrit. Those memories didn't include Necripha, however, or how she was connected to these ancient spirits.

'How did the Ancients make you? *Why* did they make you?'

Necripha was silent for a long time. So long, Uki thought she might even have died. When she spoke again, her voice was shaky and dreamlike. As if the fever was tightening its hold.

'I remember ... bits and pieces ... fragments. Being a child. Were we children? Small. Together.

Brothers and sisters, maybe ... I don't know if we were born or made. Gormalech was there. And there were others. Lots of others ...

'And then we were changed ... given jobs. I had to collect information. Store it away, organise it. A library of facts and numbers ... everything in order, everything in place. All that knowledge. All those secrets. I was so good at finding, cataloguing. Until Gormalech ruined it ...'

'Is he the one who ate the world?' Uki spoke as gently as he could, coaxing, soothing. 'The one you told me about?'

'Ate it ... yes.' Necripha's chest rattled as she fought for breath. 'All gone. Buildings. People. My library. He couldn't stop. Then everything was empty ... it was just him and me, for such a long time.'

'He covered the Earth,' said Uki, remembering the tales his mother had told him. 'He was made of living metal.'

'Metal ... yes ... but he didn't cover everything. The stories aren't quite right. The Ancients left small, shielded places. There were ruins, mountains, glaciers. He swooshed about amongst it all . . . *swish, swash* . . . you could hear him coming days before. He was easy to hide from. Hide and seek . . . can't catch me . . .'

She's feverish now, Uki thought. *She doesn't know what she's saying. Now's my chance.*

'Does he have any weakness, this Gormalech? Do any of you? Is there a secret way to destroy the things the Ancients made?'

'Never-ending . . . we . . . never . . . end. But . . . one way. Your Iffrit . . . bonded . . . became . . .'

'He bonded with me, yes. But what did he become? I don't understand what you're trying to tell me . . .'

But if there was anything else to tell, Necripha had lost the power to say it. She fell silent, only the faintest whistling of her breath telling Uki she was still alive, and even that was steadily failing.

CHAPTER THIRTEEN

Kill or Cure

The longer Uki watched Necripha, the worse he felt.

She was barely alive now. Balto was even closer to death. They both lay in the mud, only the tiny movements of their chests showing there was any kind of spark left in them.

But I could cure them. The idea came to him, popping into his head out of nowhere. *One drop of my blood and they would start to recover.*

The more he thought about it, the more he was filled with the horrid realisation that it would even be the *right* thing to do. He hadn't given them the plague. He hadn't thrown them in the pit. But if you let someone die when you knew you could save them . . . wasn't that the same as killing them?

I can't believe you're even thinking about this. His dark voice sounded amazed and disgusted. Most of the rest of him was too. But there was a fraction of Uki that felt terrible. No matter how horrible and mean Necripha and Balto were . . . surely they didn't deserve *this*?

They tried to kill you. They would do it again, if they could. They're just as evil as Charice and the others.

Yes, but he wasn't killing *them* either, was he? He was just locking them away, where they couldn't hurt anyone. If he didn't help Necripha, then she would be dead. And he would be a murderer, of a kind.

'Jori, what should I do?' He wished she was here to tell him. Although he had a good idea she would side with his dark voice. As would Kree. And Coal, probably.

And yet Jori had given up her entire future, just because she didn't want to kill. No conditions about only wanting to attack evil or mean rabbits . . . she had refused to kill *anybody*. If Necripha had been a target for her to assassinate, she wouldn't have done it. No way. Sorry. Throw me out of the clan if you must.

'I can't do it either,' Uki realised.

Whatever Necripha might be, whatever she might do to him in the future, letting her last breath gasp out without helping was the same as giving her a dose of poison.

He had to save her. He wouldn't be able to live with himself if he didn't.

Idiot.

Perhaps he was. He'd certainly feel like one if the two Endwatchers got better, turned around and then strangled him.

But there was a chance that might not happen.

A chance.

Uki walked over to them, galoshes slurping through the slime. He had no knife this time, but there was a pin at the collar of his cloak. He found the point and jabbed it into his finger, wincing, until a little bead of blood appeared, bright red against the mud.

'I don't know if you can hear me,' he said. 'But please don't hurt me when you get better. Remember what I did for you.'

He pressed his bleeding thumb to Necripha's mouth and then did the same for Balto. Then he went and crouched in the furthest corner of the pit again. And waited ...

*

It took some time for the blood to have its effect. Long enough for him to wonder if he'd been too late.

Night was beginning to fall, the sky above turning dark and the shadows at the bottom of the pit growing thicker. A heavy tiredness crept over Uki. He felt numb, exhausted ... but he didn't dare fall asleep. The terrifying thought of waking to find Balto's hands around his neck was enough to keep his eyes wide open.

Perhaps the Gurdles will rescue me, he thought. *Perhaps they're about to invade the camp right now.*

But there were no sounds of battle from outside the pit. Just the distant calls of marsh birds and the ever-present hissing of wind in the reeds.

Uki was considering whether to go and prod the

Endwatchers to see if they were dead, when Balto
let out a groan.

Here we go. This is it.

Necripha was the next to stir. She made a
coughing, retching sound in her sleep. After
that, they both began to writhe and wriggle, as
the particles of Iffrit in their system fought off
Charice's plague.

Finally, in the last few minutes of twilight, Balto
sat upright, toppling Necripha's frail body into the
mud. He flailed around with his giant arms, trying
to grab something, before scooping up a double
pawful of wet slime. He held it above his head and
squeezed, catching the droplets of filthy water in his
open mouth.

What under earth is he doing? Uki wondered,
before remembering how hungry his friends had
been when they first recovered. He had made fresh
soup for them to eat, but Balto had to make do with
stagnant swamp muck.

The big rabbit drank a few more handfuls before
realising he had dumped his mistress in the dirt. He
carefully picked her up and squeezed some slime

for her. Uki could see her cracked, wrinkled mouth lapping up the disgusting moisture. He huddled in his corner, trying to hide himself beneath his sodden cloak. Perhaps they might even have forgotten he was here ...

'So,' Necripha said, when she had lapped a mouthful or two of mud-juice. 'You did something to save us. How noble of you.'

Uki cursed. She remembered everything.

'Who are you talking to, mistress?' Balto was now well enough to stand. Uki noticed that his head reached halfway up the pit side. It was too high for Balto to leap out himself, but if Uki could get on to his shoulders ...

'The patchwork brat,' said Necripha. 'The one the fire guardian chose. He's over there, in the corner.'

Balto looked around, his beady eyes twinkling beneath his heavy brow. Uki cringed.

'Yes,' he said. 'I helped you. So maybe we can work together to get out of here?'

Necripha cackled out a raspy laugh. 'Oh, we're friends now, are we? Because you were too stupid to let us die?'

'I want his power,' said Balto. He cracked the knuckles of one hand, a finger at a time. *Snap, snap, snap, snap.* The sound echoed around the pit.

'You won't be able to get it,' said Necripha. 'Iffrit has gone. Every part of him has been given over to the child. I know that for certain now. If there was a scrap of him left, he would have stopped the fool from saving us.'

'So I'm not able to kill him?' Balto scratched his stubby ears.

'Of course you are. You can crush the life right out of him. He can't stop you without his harness. He doesn't have any power left, or he would have leaped straight out of this pit. And if he dies, whatever's left of the fire guardian will go with him.'

Uki jumped up, pressing back against the wall. It was just as he feared and now there was nowhere to run. 'But . . . but . . . I *saved* you!' he shouted. 'And what about Charice? We could stop her together!'

'Charice,' repeated Balto. 'She made us sick.'

'Forget about her,' said Necripha. She had struggled to her feet and was leaning against the muddy wall for support. 'She's too far gone to be any good to us. We shall go to Mortix and persuade her to join us instead. Then we can crush the weakened Gormalech together. After that we can destroy the goddesses, and then pick off all the remaining leftovers of the Ancients at our leisure. Charice will get what's coming to her eventually.'

'And the brat?' Balto looked over at Uki, a smile beginning to spread across his face.

'Kill him,' said Necripha. 'He's no threat any more, but it will be one less thing to worry about.'

'Good,' said Balto. 'I like killing.'

With both meaty paws outstretched, he began to stalk across the pit towards Uki.

I told you this would happen.

Uki tensed his leg muscles, shook his head to clear it. This wasn't the time for voices, he needed to *think*.

Balto was big, yes. And very strong. But he had only just recovered from the deadly plague. He would be weaker, dizzier ... maybe even slower. And he would be expecting Uki to just stand there, frozen in terror while he stomped towards him.

Not likely, Uki thought.

He made a dash towards the huge rabbit, ducking

at the last minute and scampering between his legs. Balto swiped for him and missed, leaving Uki to sprint across the pit to the other side.

The huge rabbit simply turned around and started walking towards him again.

You're in a pit, stupid. Running away won't help. You can't do it all night, can you?

Night. It was nearly dark. Even if Uki *could* keep dodging, he would tire out eventually. And then when he slept . . .

He looked again at how tall Balto was. How a leap from his shoulders might just make the edge of the pit . . .

Uki was weaker without the crystals, true, but he still had the power that Iffrit had given him. He was much stronger and quicker than an ordinary rabbit. And that was something Necripha and Balto didn't realise. They thought he had nothing without the harness. That they could snuff him out in a blink.

I'm going to have to let him grab me, Uki thought. *He'll lift me up to try and kill me, and then I need to slip free somehow . . .*

Uki got ready for another dash, his galoshes slipping in the wet slime on the pit floor.

Slime . . .

As Balto neared, he ran again, this time diving flat on his face between the big rabbit's legs. He made sure he rolled and wiggled in the soggy muck, and then paused for a fraction of a second – long enough for Balto to grab his leg.

'Got you!'

Balto heaved him up with one paw, and then grabbed Uki's collar with the other. He slammed him up against the pit wall, hard enough to make sparks dance in front of Uki's eyes.

'Killing time!' Balto drew back a fist, ready to pound Uki into muddy paste, but, as Uki had thought, his movements were slow and laboured, his body drained and famished from fighting for its life.

By digging his back paws into the muddy wall, Uki was able to find enough purchase to kick upwards, yanking his slippery cloak and shirt from Balto's grasp.

His push took him high, smacking into the face

and shoulders of the big rabbit, who staggered backwards in surprise.

Uki dug deep, drawing on the fiery energy of Iffrit that kept him alive. He could sense each beat of his heart as it pumped a surge of adrenaline through him. He could feel all the muscles in Balto's chunky neck as his feet found footholds, as his paws gripped the fat rabbit's ears and fur.

Quick as a flame, he clambered up on to Balto's head, balancing on it for a moment as if it were a stepping stone in a lake. Then, with all the power in his legs, he kicked off, shooting up through the air, arms outstretched.

He cleared the lip of the pit easily, half slipping through a gap in the crude wooden grille over the top. He hung there for a moment, scrabbling at the lashed-together branches, with his legs still dangling. For a few awful seconds, he thought Balto might grab one of his feet and pull him back in, but he gripped one branch with his paw, then another.

Using his arms, he hauled himself out until his feet were clear and he could scramble across to the safety of the pit edge. From down below he could hear a spattering of wet slaps and slithers and the bubbly roar of a very large, very angry rabbit being dunked in wet mud.

Balto must have been kicked to the ground with the force of Uki's leap. *I must have more strength than I realised*, Uki thought. *Even without the crystals.*

'Curse you, you little brat!'

Necripha's cries echoed up from the pit. She might have been cured of the disease, but being stuck down there without food or water . . . she would soon end up the same as that poor old skeleton.

And Uki wouldn't make the mistake of saving her twice. Allowing himself a little smile of triumph, he turned his back on the pit and ran off into the night.

INTERLUDE

T he bard pauses in his tale and stands up to stretch. He smacks his lips and nudges the embers of their smoky campfire with a piece of old table leg.

'Why have you stopped?' Rue asks. He is lying on his stomach in a nest of blankets, from which he has been staring up at the bard, lost in the world of Uki. 'It's only midday. There must be loads of the story left to tell.'

'Oh, there is,' says the bard. 'I was just thinking that a spot of chamomile tea would be nice. Perhaps you'd like to get the fire going again and boil me up some water.'

'Not really,' says Rue. 'I want to hear how Uki escapes the Maggitch camp.'

'You misunderstood me,' says the bard. 'It was an order, disguised as a question. Tea first, story later.'

Rue, muttering under his breath, heaves himself up and begins walking around the ruined tower, collecting an armful of broken wooden furniture that is dry enough to burn. He casts a few glances over at Jori, who is sitting at her lookout post, carefully sharpening her sword with a whetstone she has taken from an embroidered leather pouch.

As he brings the kindling back to the fire and begins to stack it in a pyramid, he clears his throat and asks her a question. 'Would you have done it? Left Necripha to die, I mean. Or would you have saved her like Uki did?'

Jori looks up at him for a long while, her intense grey gaze more than a little intimidating.

'That,' she says, 'is a difficult question. I'd like to think I would have saved her, if I had the power. But considering everything that happened because of her ... perhaps it would have been better to let her die.'

'What happened? What did she do? Did she escape as well? How?'

'Now look what you've done,' says the bard. 'I'm never going to get my tea now. You can only feed him tiny bits of information at a time, and absolutely, definitely don't give away *any* hints whatsoever.'

'I'm sorry.' Jori laughs. 'I didn't mean to set him off. He's like one of those clockwork toys they make in Eisenfell. Wind up the spring and he's away.'

'Don't laugh at me!' Rue stands with paws on hips, the fire forgotten. 'These are important questions! I need to know these things for my training!'

'Let *me* worry about your training ...' says the bard, but he is interrupted by Jori suddenly raising a finger.

'Shh!' she says. 'Did you hear that?'

The bard and Rue freeze, ears pricked. At first Rue can't hear anything except the cawing of a distant crow, but then he detects a soft rustling sound. Muffled, coming from within the tower.

'The library,' he whispers. 'I think there's something down there.'

Jori leaps from the rubble, her sharpened sword

at the ready. Like a wildcat padding after her prey, she slinks across the floor to the open trapdoor and crouches, listening.

More rustling.

Jori glances at the bard, wide-eyed, and then drops down into the Endwatch library below.

'We have to help her!' Rue hisses, and dashes over too. He is stopped by the bard grabbing hold of his cloak hood, but not before he has got his head into the cellar hole. He peers into the darkness, upside down, and sees Jori amongst the shadows, glimmers of light flashing from her sword blade.

'Stop where you are!' she shouts, and Rue sees there is another rabbit, over in the far corner. It is dressed in a black cloak, making it look like a moving shadow. Between it and Jori is a pile of torn scrolls and manuscripts, and it is clutching something in its paws. As Jori draws closer, there is a shower of bright orange sparks, some of which hit the jumble of ancient parchment, flowering into flames.

'No!' Jori yells. She leaps over the burning scrolls, sword slashing, but the intruder is already on the move. It cries out as the sword catches it somewhere, and flings a handful of books into Jori's face. As she staggers backwards, the cloaked rabbit disappears down a hidden passage.

'Goddess curse you!' Jori shouts, and runs after it. Rue pulls against the bard's grip, trying to struggle free.

'Hold still!' the bard tells him. 'It's too dangerous!'

'There's fire!' Rue shouts back. 'We have to put it out!'

'Hern's horns!' The bard lets go of Rue's hood, sending him toppling down into the cellar. A stack of old books breaks his fall. A few seconds later, and the bard comes slipping down the ladder. He hauls Rue up and they run over to the burning manuscripts, stamping at the flames and flapping them with their cloaks.

Luckily, the pieces of tattered books and scrolls are more than a little damp and the fire hasn't taken hold. A few frantic minutes of panic, and the sparks have all been put out, leaving a mist of pungent smoke and two panting rabbits.

'Where did Jori go?' the bard asks, peering around the dingy cellar.

'There was an Endwatch rabbit in here,' says Rue. 'Jori chased it up a tunnel over there.'

He points to a place in the darkness where there is a shadow deeper than those around it. A hidden passageway that they missed in all the searches.

The bard and Rue stare at it, waiting for Jori to come back, clutching each other's paws, breath held tight.

Nothing happens for what seems like an eternity. Finally, there is a crunching, *whomping* sound. A cloud of chalky dust bursts from the tunnel into the cellar.

'Jori!' Rue cries. He sprints to the passage, but the bard holds him back again.

'There must have been a collapse in the tunnel,' he says. 'It's not safe.'

'But Jori!' Rue sobs. 'She's stuck up there! We have to dig her out!'

'No need.' A dusty face suddenly appears in the entrance, followed by the rest of Jori, covered head to paw in cobwebs, chalk and clumps of mud.

'Clarion's lute pegs!' cries the bard, rushing to help her. He pulls her arm over his shoulder and, with a little help from Rue, they walk her away from the tunnel, over to the cellar ladder.

'What happened?' Rue asks, when she has had a few seconds to cough and sneeze all the dust out of her nose.

'Damned Endwatch,' Jori says, rubbing grit out of her eyes. 'They had a secret way into the library after all. I must have walked past it three times or more. Looks like they were going to burn all the books and smoke us out.'

'We stopped the fire,' says Rue. 'It was too damp to burn much, anyway.'

'Well done.' Jori ruffles his ears. 'I nearly got the sneak-weasel who did it, but they'd set a trap down there. Whole tunnel crashed around my whiskers. I managed to dodge it, but the passage is completely blocked now. No way out.'

'I bet he wouldn't have got away if you'd had your potion,' says Rue, scowling.

'There wasn't time to take it,' says Jori. 'But you're right. And we might have been able to escape.'

'Don't worry about that now,' says the bard. 'At

least you're safe, and they didn't smoke us out. All we have to do is sit tight. The Foxguard will be here soon enough, I'm sure.'

Rue and Jori both nod. They make their way back up the ladder, where Rue manages to get their campfire burning and the water boiling for some badly needed tea. But all the while they each keep a nervous eye on the open door to the cellar. That dark, musty room that could be crawling with secret traps and tunnels.

*

It is the bard who suggests continuing the story of Uki. He can see Rue is shaken up: legs curled against his chest and ears twitching at the slightest rustle. *Living through life-threatening peril for the first time must be difficult*, the bard thinks. *It's not so bad when you've seen it on a regular basis. Since before you could walk, even.*

'Oh yes,' says Rue. 'That would be nice.'

'We're getting to the good bit now, Rue,' says Jori, trying to perk him up. 'The epic battle at the end. Always my favourite part.'

'Do you take your dusk potion?' Rue asks,

his ears twitching up. 'Do you do some amazing battle skills?'

'All my skills are amazing,' says Jori, smiling. 'And I think I'm going to need some potion to deal with what the Maggitches have in store.'

'Ooh! What have they got? Seven-headed snapping turtles? Giant, diseased snakes? Hordes of pus-dripping frogs?'

'Now, now,' says the bard. 'Don't get carried away. This is a *true* story, remember. Besides, Uki has to get out of the enemy camp first. And he still doesn't have his crystal harness ...'

CHAPTER FOURTEEN

Crispy Maggots

The night sky above the Maggitch camp was cloudy, moonless. Uki could see shadowy outlines of huts and tents about him. Here and there were bare, twisted trees and straggly shapes that might be bushes. One or two thin lines of light were visible – the cracks of doorways or windows – but no torches or lanterns shone outside.

This is a smugglers' den, Uki reminded himself. *Or at least it was. It's designed to be invisible from the Shrikes.* A campfire or lantern would be an instant giveaway.

Uki moved into the cover of a broad, crumbling tree. He could smell the damp, rotting wood and the earthy scent of the fungi that were eating it.

On instinct, he pressed his right, white-furred side against the trunk, knowing it would as good as glow in the night, making him a target. But when he looked at his arms, both were covered in a thick coating of mud. He was finally all one colour, ears to paws. A dirty mud-grey, like a scoop of the swamp had come to life and started stalking about the fen.

Uki gazed out at that mass of waterways and reeds. Somewhere amongst it all were his friends. He desperately wanted to run out to them, to get away from this sickening mound, but he couldn't. Not yet. Not without his harness and the crystals.

Where were his friends, though? Had they been captured, like him? Or had they fought off the Glopstickers? And if they had, how would he ever find them again in this darkness? He would have to worry about that later. First, his weapons.

He looked again at the silhouettes of the buildings. There were at least ten, and any of them could be hiding his things. Or something worse. And there could be dozens more huts or burrows hidden around the mound.

If he waited until daylight, he would be spotted, mud coating or not. But perhaps there was another way. Iffrit's senses allowed him to track the escaped spirits ... might they be able to find the trapped ones?

He could only try.

Sitting with his back to the spongy wood of the tree, Uki closed his eyes and focused. He slowed his breathing and tried to think of nothing else but the spirits and their location.

It was difficult. Being this close to Charice, all he could feel was the ebb and flow of her power. Pulses of sickly green energy that made his stomach clench.

Focus. See beneath all that.

He tried to let it wash over him. He imagined his mind splitting in two, becoming another rabbit looking down on himself, inspecting everything the original Uki sensed and felt. Sifting out each tiny detail.

There ... at the edge of his mind ... was that something? A hint, a taste: purple and spiky, the smell of musty libraries and ancient dust.

Necripha, he realised. *Still frothing with anger at his escape.*

The two trapped spirits would be fainter than that, he knew. Stuck behind the crystal walls of their prisons, battering against them like moths around a lantern.

He breathed slower, went deeper, searching and searching until . . .

There! Twin flickers of red and yellow. A kind of humming vibration that he recognised. It was Valkus and Gaunch. They were nearby and muffled by their crystals, but without the bonding power of Iffrit around them they were becoming bolder, stronger.

I have to be quick, Uki told himself. *Before they escape again.* Then his quest really would be over.

He hopped up and began to follow the trace of the crystals like a wolf after its supper. Keeping low to the ground, squinting through the murky darkness, he made his way to one of the huts. A timber-framed thing with walls of packed mud and a roof of straw, it was half hidden by a bank of nettles and ivy. There were no windows, but it did have a wooden door, loosely fitted on hinges made of rope.

Uki pressed a paw to it, then an ear. The sense of the spirits was a fraction stronger here – they were definitely inside – and better still, the hut seemed silent. No voices or movement.

It sounds empty, he thought, as he put a shoulder to the wood and gently pushed, hoping he wasn't about to stumble into a den of slumbering Maggitch warriors.

No soldiers, thank the Goddess.

An empty hut, with two glass lanterns hanging from the rafters. In the centre, three squat wooden barrels, with piles of smaller kegs stacked up around the walls.

As Uki carefully shut the door behind him, he could hear a rustling, slithering sound. Or rather thousands of sounds, as they overlapped and ran into each other. Like a hundred straw nests of wiggling mice or . . .

Maggots! All three barrels were filled almost to the brim with seething, twitching bodies. Countless pale, fleshy grubs wriggling over one another and a sickly sweet stench of something they were eating. Long-dead meat or spoiled food. It made Uki want to retch.

This must be the next batch of flies, Uki realised. Among the white bodies he could see many had already begun to cocoon themselves in hard brown casing. The armoured, six-legged shells of dragonfly nymphs crawled, looking for a spot to climb out and hatch. A few more days and they would emerge as a cloud of deadly flying insects, ready to deliver Charice's plague on another unsuspecting town or warren.

Uki edged past, deciding to burn the barrels on his way out. If he ever managed to escape, that is.

There was a doorway on the opposite side of the hut, covered by a piece of dirty sacking. He lifted it aside a fraction and peered through.

A tunnel lay beyond, sloping at a steep angle under the earth, into the mound. The crystals were down there somewhere, and so was Charice. Uki put a paw to his head. There could be endless loops of tunnels inside the hill. What if he ran into Charice before he had his harness? Without a spear, he couldn't even scratch her.

Standing here won't harm her either, said his dark voice. **Stop being a coward and get on with it.**

But I am a coward, Uki thought. *Facing another spirit terrifies me. I don't think I could do it on my own, even if I did have my crystals.*

Still, he managed to put a paw inside the tunnel, then another. With gritted teeth, he headed down inside the mound.

It was the first time he'd been inside a proper burrow, but his mother had been a warren-dwelling rabbit, and living under the ground was in his bones. He found the solid, packed earth around him comforting. The dangling roots, the peaty, crumbly smell. The tracks of earthworms in the walls.

Oil lamps were burning in alcoves down the tunnel. A warm orange light that might have been cosy, if Uki hadn't been expecting an armed Maggitch to jump out at any moment. After a steep climb down, the tunnel levelled out and then came to a T-junction, where he could turn left or right.

Uki stopped, crouching low, and edged his muddy head around the corner, pleased to see his coated fur was exactly the same colour as the earthen walls.

Nothing to the left, but a few metres down on the

right was a rabbit. He was standing still, guarding the entrance to a chamber.

That means something important is inside, Uki thought. He could sense the faint tendrils of energy he had been following. Could it be the crystals?

Uki took a good look at the guard. He was tall but hunched, his head covered in a hooded snakeskin cloak. Beneath it, Uki glimpsed patches of swollen flesh. Angry clusters of red boils hung down from the guard's chin, and his eyes were puffed up into narrow slits. Crusted ooze dribbled like melted candlewax from his nose and mouth, and Uki could hear a wet, wheezing sound as he breathed.

He's in the grip of Charice's plague, Uki thought. *But does that mean he'll be weak enough for me to beat?*

He remembered the rabbits who had attacked the Gurdle village. There was nothing weak or vulnerable about *them*. No, charging down the tunnel and attacking the guard was a stupid idea. He needed some kind of distraction to get him away from the door.

That was when he thought of the maggot barrels.

Two turnips on one stalk, Uki thought. He was back in the hut, listening to the quiet, squirmy rustling of the maggots. His eyes roamed around the other barrels in the room. Smaller kegs, stacked everywhere, marked up in Hulst runes and other forms of writing he'd never seen before.

Smugglers' booty. Wine and rum, probably, but there had to be other goodies too. Uki had noticed all the lamps everywhere. They needed oil to burn – nut oil, seed oil; his mother had even told him of ships that sailed out into the icy waters to hunt giant sea beasts and make oil from their fat.

He spotted a keg with a squiggle painted on that looked something like a flame. Lifting it down, he pulled out the cork bung and sniffed: a strong, fishy odour that burned his eyes. When he shook the keg, he could hear the liquid sloshing inside. A thick, gloopy sound. It was definitely oil.

Uki heaved the keg on to his shoulder and began to pour the oil into one of the barrels. It sloshed all over the teeming grubs, sinking down into the depths, covering them with its shiny slickness. They seemed to sense that something was wrong and

255

began to wriggle even faster. Uki was worried that some of the chrysalises might pop, although they would probably be too thickly coated in oil to fly.

He threw the empty keg aside and cracked open another. Into the barrels it went; a soupy, fishy, maggoty mess. When he was sure that every last plague-bearing grub had been covered, he went back to the booty around the walls and made a gap to hide in, as close to the tunnel entrance as possible. Then he took one of the lanterns down from above.

'Here goes,' he said to himself. He dropped the flaming lamp into one of the barrels and jumped back.

He had half expected the barrel to explode, but instead a large, steady flame appeared, quickly growing to fill the barrel top. It flickered up to the rafters, flooding the hut with blazing light. Uki had created a giant lamp, with whale-oil fuel and maggots for the wick. They began to sizzle and pop, giving off a rancid, burnt stink.

There weren't the clouds of smoke he'd been hoping for, but the blaze and the smell might be enough to attract attention. Uki tore the sacking from the tunnel doorway, held it to the burning barrel and then used it to light the other two. When all three were blazing merrily, he ran to his cubbyhole and hid.

The stench of crisping maggots filled his lungs and made his eyes sting. He wrapped his damp, muddy cloak over his mouth, trying to breathe as little as possible.

It wasn't long before the guard in the tunnel noticed it too. Uki heard his footsteps approaching. He was making gargling, grunting noises as he tried to sound the alarm through his swollen, blistered throat.

Eyes watering, Uki waited until the guard blundered into the hut. As he'd hoped, the Maggitch rabbit ran straight to the barrels, panicking about his precious creatures being turned into a barbecue.

Seizing his chance, Uki slipped out of his hiding place and ran down the tunnel to the now unguarded chamber. It had a flimsy wooden door made out of planks of worm-eaten wood, which swung open when Uki pushed it. He entered a dark chamber.

Dark, except for two spots of coloured light that glowed on a table in the centre. Red and yellow – the crystals that held Gaunch and Valkus.

Uki ran to grab them, finding them still slotted into his harness. His three remaining spears were on the table too, crusted in dried mud but unbroken.

Fingers trembling, he pulled off his muddy, sodden cloak. It was torn to shreds, he saw, past saving. With a twinge of regret, he dropped it to the ground and pulled the harness over his head, feeling the leather straps fall into their usual places, filling the gaps that had felt so empty.

As soon as the crystals were back on his chest, he felt Iffrit's energy ripple through him again, covering the trapped spirits in their prisons, knitting their bindings tight. All his strength came bubbling back. His muscles felt like they might pop, his legs were like springs of Eisenfell steel, his senses sharp as Jori's swishing sword.

He'd become so used to these feelings, it wasn't until he'd lost them that he remembered how strong the crystals had made him. Why hadn't he been more confident? Why hadn't he charged at Charice when he'd had the chance?

But he had the chance now.

He snatched up his spears, slotting two into his harness, holding the third ready in his paws. Marching back to the door, he pulled it open and stepped out into the corridor ... only to be met by a terrifying sight that made his new confidence evaporate like marsh mist.

Charging along the tunnel from deep in Gollop's Mound was a horde of angry rabbits.

Except they didn't really look much like rabbits any more. Riddled with disease, like the guard had been, their faces were hidden beneath swellings and streams of gunk. They filled the whole tunnel as they scrabbled their way up, their ruined paws leaving streaks of poisoned blood on the earthen walls. Only the odd scrap of snakeskin clothing showed they had once been Maggitches.

Uki stared, frozen. He hadn't imagined there would be so many. There was no way he could fight them all, not even with his renewed strength. He would end up stripped of his harness again, and thrown back in the pit with Balto and Necripha.

But there was a chance to escape. If he could get to the tunnel junction before them, he could run up and out through the hut. He could get back to the Gurdle village and bring them here … with their help he might be able to hold off the Maggitches long enough to find Charice. And if he was quick about it, there might not be any bloodshed.

The thought of seeing his friends again gave him the push he needed. He put his head down and sprinted at the oncoming creatures, flying down the tunnel like an arrow from a bow.

Closer, closer he came to the horde … close enough to smell the stink of disease pouring off them. Close enough for the rabbits at the front to spot him through their swollen eyelids.

'Intruder! Intruder!' came their garbled shouts, and they reached out for him with their bloated paws. But at the last second, when he was just about to crash into their grasp, he swerved left and pelted up the tunnel. He had reached the turning with half a whisker to spare.

Uki wasn't safe yet, though. He could hear the screams from the crowd behind him as they turned the corner themselves and started following him up the slope. It was only their numbers that slowed them down, crammed in the tunnel like ripe blueberries in a wine press.

And there were more up ahead.

As Uki cleared the tunnel and burst into the hut, he could see the guard had got help. There were at least five Maggitches, all standing around the burning barrels, flapping at them with blankets and their snakeskin cloaks. Smoke *was* everywhere now, and the choking stink of burnt wood, fish oil and cooked maggot. The scene was so chaotic that Uki was able to blunder through them all before they even knew he was there.

He barged the Maggitches out of his path, sending them flying into each other and the smouldering tubs of dead maggots. They tumbled about the room, knocking kegs over, smashing the barrels and sending sprays of charred filth everywhere. Through it all shot Uki, straight out of the hut door and into the blissful fresh night air.

Still, he wasn't safe. The alarm had been raised and more Maggitches were outside, these ones ready with spears and bows, suspecting their camp was under attack. They turned at the sound of the hut door crashing open and had a brief glimpse of Uki, framed in the lamplight, before he was amongst them, ducking and weaving as he sprinted out of the camp.

One or two got off a shot and Uki heard the whistle of arrows *zipping* past his head. But his coating of mud made him hard to spot, and he was soon out of the cluster of huts, in between the straggly clumps of nettles and brambles.

The ground sloped steeply downwards towards the marsh and was dotted with holes, roots and trailing vines. Still running at speed, Uki stumbled once, twice and then found himself tumbling, ears over tail, bouncing down the side of the mound like a child's ball.

Crump, crump, crump! His body was jarred as he spilled over and over, finally crashing to a stop in a cluster of hawthorn bushes. Somehow, his spear was still clutched in his paw, although his head was spinning too much to use it.

He was trying to untangle himself when he felt the front of his harness being grabbed. A strong paw had hold of him, yanking him upwards to where a single fierce eye gleamed out of a scarred pink face.

'Got one!' he heard his captor shout and, from the corner of his eye, he glimpsed a large metal hammer beginning its swing downwards through the air, towards his head.

CHAPTER FIFTEEN

Beneath Gollop's Mound

'Coal! NO!' Uki shouted, raising a paw, trying to block the hammer speeding at him. 'It's me! It's Uki!'

There was a flicker in Coal's gaze, a tremor in his arm. He swerved the blow at the last second and it whistled past Uki's face, making his whiskers tremble.

The strong fist gripping Uki's jerkin tightened and he was lifted higher in the air as Coal stared him up and down. Uki knew he wouldn't be recognised straight away. His distinctive patchwork fur was hidden under claggy half-dried mud. He could quite easily have knocked Coal's hand away, but he didn't want to hurt his friend with his newly returned strength. Instead, he waved a paw.

'The harness . . .' he said, pointing at the buckle on his chest. 'The crystals.'

Coal's eye instantly widened, and he dropped Uki like a hot potato.

'Bless my whiskers! I nearly knocked a hole in your head! I'm so sorry!'

'That's . . . all right . . .' Uki said, catching his breath. The flight from the tunnel, the hut, the fall . . . it had all happened in the space of a minute. He was only just beginning to recover when two other furry bodies jumped on top of him, spilling him to the ground.

'Uki, you're alive!' Kree was hugging him around the waist, while Jori squeezed his shoulders.

'Thank Kether!' she said. 'We managed to fight off those Maggitch Glopsticker-things, but I saw you go under the mud . . .'

'I'm fine,' said Uki, picking himself up again. Just when he thought the welcomes were over, a huge pink tongue suddenly slapped against the side of his face. Mooka had bounded up next to him and was licking him with great affection.

'Ugh!' Uki tried to push the jerboa away. 'What is he doing?'

'He's pleased to see you,' said Kree. 'He knows you saved his life.'

'Does he?' Uki wasn't sure that was true, but he gave Mooka a quick cuddle, just the same, before turning back to his friends. 'I didn't expect you to be here. Did you come on your own?'

'We's all here,' said a voice from somewhere in the dark. He recognised it as Ma Gurdle. 'We's come for the muckle gurt reckoning.'

Uki squinted across the darkened fen and thought he could make out the shadowy shapes of many rabbits, all cloaked and crouching low. He could see the odd glimmer of a spearhead or arrow, but from up on the mound the whole force was invisible.

'Rawnie took us straight back to the village,' Jori explained. 'We raised the alarm, and we all came here. We were going to attack at dawn.'

'I think we might need to act before then,' said

Uki. 'I've a feeling the whole Maggitch clan is about to come charging down on top of us.'

'Why?' asked Kree. 'What happened to you?'

In few words, Uki told them about the pit and Necripha. He described the vats of larvae and the tunnels inside Gollop's Mound.

'Roasted maggots? I wondered what you stank of,' said Kree, wrinkling her nose. 'I thought it was the crusty slime all over you. That smells too.'

'Well, I'm very sorry,' said Uki, pointing up the hill with his spear. 'But I haven't had time for a bath. Now we must get back into the tunnels to find Charice.'

'What about this Necripha?' Coal asked. 'Is she still in the pit you spoke of?'

'Why are you asking about *her*?' Jori scowled at the smith. 'She can stay there and rot for all we care. Our mission is to get the spirit.'

'Do you think the Gurdles can cause a diversion?' Uki said. 'There were too many Maggitches to deal with on my own, but if they are busy fighting, I might be able to slip through.'

'I think the dilly-version be coming to us,' said

Ma Gurdle. She nodded to the top of the mound where the Maggitches had banded together. They held lanterns and flaming torches to see by, and they were about to come storming down the hill after Uki.

'They don't know we're here,' Jori said. 'We can take them by surprise.'

'Weapons ready,' Ma Gurdle hissed to her troops. 'If you could give them Maggitches a bit of persuasion, Uki . . .'

'Excuse me?' Uki stared at the patch of darkness that Ma Gurdle's voice had come from. 'Persuasion?'

'She means act as bait,' said Kree. 'Like a fat worm left out on the plain for the buzzards.'

'Oh,' said Uki. 'I see.'

Not really liking the idea, he walked a little up the hillside and then lay down in as crumpled a heap as he could. 'Aargh!' he shouted. 'My leg!'

'Put some effort into it,' Jori hissed. 'That wouldn't fool anybody!'

'Neeargh! The pain!' Uki rolled around for a moment, then popped his head up to check. The bobbing lanterns and torches were beginning to weave down the hill towards him. He gave a bit more of a wiggle, just enough to be spotted. The Maggitches took the bait and started charging down the slope.

'Hold,' he heard Ma Gurdle whispering. 'Hold till they're nearly upon us.'

Realising that meant *after* the Maggitches had reached him, Uki got up and then began to hobble with a fake limp, leading them down into the flat marshland, in amongst the reeds and hawthorns. The Maggitches were only too pleased to follow, and began cheering garbled cries of victory, waving their weapons and torches as they came.

Uki kept going, on past the bushes, until his galoshes began to sink in the soggy ground. Then he ducked behind one of the last remaining trees. The Maggitches halted, looking angrily around for him.

And that was when the Gurdles charged.

With a chorus of wild whoops, they burst from their hiding places, falling on the startled Maggitches before they could react. Many were knocked to the ground even as they raised their weapons to defend themselves. Others fell back to the mound, screaming in terror. The sight made Uki wince. *They thought the Gurdles were all dead*, he realised. *They must have no idea what's going on.* He had wanted to avoid all this. It almost made him feel sorry for the Maggitches.

'Quickly, Uki! Now's our chance!' Jori had run up beside him, along with Kree and Coal.

'Climb on to Mooka's back,' said Kree. 'He can carry us up the hill. Not you though, Coal. You're too fat.'

'Charming,' said Coal, as he helped Jori clamber on to the jerboa. Uki leaped up, enjoying the sensation of having all his power again.

'Hai, Mooka!' Kree shouted. 'Hai! Hai!'

The jerboa sprang forwards, bursting out of the bush and bounding across the battlefield. As soon as he had solid ground beneath his paws, he began to tear up the hillside, dodging the fleeing Maggitches and the Gurdles that were chasing them.

Uki looked over his shoulder to see Coal puffing along behind them. The hill was too steep for him to use his crutch properly and he kept having to pause to knock a Maggitch or two out of the way with his hammer.

Mooka soon cleared all the scrub and reached the top of Gollop's Mound. Uki pointed over to the huts, the one he had visited still pouring smoke from its doorway. 'There! Inside that one is a tunnel down into the mound.'

Kree steered Mooka over and they climbed off his back. Jori drew her sword, checking around for any remaining Maggitch warriors.

'Mooka won't fit through the tunnel,' Uki said. 'We'll have to leave him here.'

Kree looked horrified. 'But I want to go with you this time. I want to fight the spirit!'

Just as Jori was beginning to argue, the panting, staggering figure of Coal appeared at the edge of the camp. He came straight over to them, fighting for breath. 'I . . . can . . . stay with the jerboa,' he gasped. 'Keep . . . the way out . . . clear for you.'

'Really?' Kree squeezed his arm. 'That would be very kind of you.'

'Not . . . a problem,' Coal said, wheezing out each word. 'I can't go on . . . any further . . . anyway.'

'Then let's get on with it,' said Jori. 'Before those Maggitches come back up the hill.'

Uki nodded. He shifted his spear to grip it in both paws and took a deep breath of air, ready to step into the smoky hut. Kree did the same and Jori unclipped her flask of dusk potion, taking a deep swig.

'Onwards,' she said, and they plunged into the smoke.

Even though he had been in the hut before, the stink still made Uki gag. The fires in the barrels had been put out, leaving a smouldering heap of charred mess in the middle of the room. Squinting through the smoke, Uki headed straight for the tunnel entrance. Behind him, he could hear Jori and Kree spluttering and coughing.

As they ran down the tunnel slope, the air cleared. By the time they reached the junction at the bottom, they could see and breathe normally again.

'Which way?' Jori asked. The dusk potion made her movements quick and jerky. Birdlike, almost.

Uki didn't have to focus hard. Charice was angry and seething. He could feel waves of furious energy pulsing out from the centre of the mound.

'Left,' he said, leading the way.

The passage ran straight for a few metres, the

walls still scarred by the Maggitches' charge earlier. It came to a steep staircase, the steps carved out of the earth itself. Just as they had begun to descend, a Maggitch appeared, clambering towards them.

'Allow me,' said Jori. She stepped in front of Uki and then moved so quickly he couldn't even see her actions. There was the sound of her sword swishing through the air, and in the next blink the Maggitch collapsed to the floor. The spear it had been holding was sliced into tiny pieces and there was an egg-sized lump on its head, in amongst all the boils and pustules.

'Never attack someone upwards on a staircase,' Jori said, already stepping over her victim and heading down the steps.

They were challenged three more times, and each Maggitch was quickly knocked out by Jori. It seemed nearly all of Charice's soldiers had been sent out after Uki. She must have thought herself safe in her hideout, with all the Gurdles dead in their village.

After running along several narrow tunnels and down another flight of steps, they came to a wide double door. Lanterns burned in alcoves on either side, and a sickly, pungent smell seeped through the cracks, choking up the tunnel.

'*Mik jibbadan lashki!*' Kree pulled her cloak up over her mouth and nose. 'What is that *stink*?'

'It smells like the barrels of maggots did,' said Uki. 'Only much, much worse.'

Jori had covered her nose as well. She stood at the doorway, ready to kick it open. 'Is it Charice?' she asked. 'Is she inside?'

Uki nodded. The force of her power was stronger than ever. Even with Iffrit's immunity, he was finding it hard to stand. He lifted his spear, ready to throw, to get the crystal close enough so that it could draw her in and trap her. He gave Jori a nod. She nodded back and sent a spinning kick into the doors that splintered them off the hinges, revealing the chamber within.

Uki stepped through, ready to hurl his spear straight away this time. He wouldn't give Charice a split second to unleash another cloud of flies to stop him.

Except she was nowhere to be seen.

The circular room had an island of earth in the centre, empty except for a crude chair made of lashed-together branches and scraps of snakeskin.

Around it, in a ring, was a ditch filled to the brim with the source of the putrid stink. Larvae. More than there had been in the barrels. More than Uki could ever have imagined. Millions upon millions of them, writhing and seething. Fat white ones, tiny pink and brown ones. Mealworms, bloodworms, threadlike twitching mosquito larvae. They crawled over each other in an endless sea.

Here and there, bits of their dinner surfaced before sinking back down into the seething mess. Pieces of rotten meat, some with flaps of skin still attached. Frogs, toads, newts ... even a rat's tail and other fragments of fur that could have been weasels, badgers or worse ... rabbits.

'Where is she?' Jori asked. 'My potion won't last much longer. We need to find her!'

'I think,' said Uki, wincing. 'I think she's in *there* somewhere.'

They moved closer to the ditch, looking down into the sea of bubbling larvae. The sight, combined with the stench and the overpowering sense of Charice herself, was making Uki feel horribly sick. He could see Kree was suffering as well. Jori seemed to be coping better, but that was probably due to the potion she had taken.

'What do we do? Dive in and search for her?' Kree gave the maggot ditch a poke with her spear. It was very deep.

Uki thought hard. Climbing into *that* seemed crazy. Maybe even dangerous. Who knew what those twisted grubs would do to living flesh, and being eaten alive by a hundred thousand tiny jaws was not his idea of fun.

Then he remembered the barrels.

'We could set fire to them,' he said. 'That would drive her out if she's hiding there.'

'Good idea,' said Jori. In a twitch, she dashed back to the doorway and fetched one of the lanterns. She emptied the oil out into the ditch and then dropped the lantern in. A puddle of fire instantly appeared, and the larvae surrounding it went crazy, trying to wriggle away from the flames.

'There are barrels of oil up in the hut,' Uki said.

He was about to suggest running back to fetch it, when he felt a surge of Charice's power. A blast of sickness that made every cell in his body clench up. Even with all his strength, it was enough to make him stagger. Kree and Jori both clutched their stomachs and then toppled forwards, tumbling into the ditch.

'No!' Uki shouted. He ran forwards to grab them, but they sank under the surface quicker than he could move. He plunged his arms in amongst the squirming grubs and groped around, trying to ignore the tickling, seething, wriggling sensation. But his paws found nothing. His friends had been dragged deep down, out of his grasp.

'Charice!' he screamed. 'Give them back! I know you can hear me!'

Looking across the chamber, he tried to spot some sign of the spirit, or the body of Granny Maggitch it was hiding inside. If he could capture it quickly, maybe the maggots would release Kree and Jori.

It seemed hopeless, but then a ripple appeared. Like a slowly building ocean wave, it rose on the far side of the room and began travelling over to him. Something was pushing the larvae up from underneath, sending them tumbling to the sides of the pit as it passed.

Uki readied his spear and stepped into a throwing stance. He gathered all his strength, all his energy and held it tight, ready to unleash. As soon as Charice breached the surface . . .

There was an explosion of tiny, wriggling worm bodies as something huge burst upwards, out from the bottom of the ditch.

Uki sensed it rising, up and up and up – much bigger than a rabbit, more solid than a spirit. He lunged forwards with his spear, even as his sight was clouded by thousands of scattered maggots. There was a solid *thud* as it connected with something fleshy . . .

. . . and then the larvae fell away, revealing his target.

Not Charice. Not Granny Maggitch.

He had struck an adder. A big one. Rearing up, almost to the ceiling, it was clearly in the clutches of Charice's disease. The thing had gaping open sores all over its body and its eyes were blinded by dripping pus. Its mouth was choked with ulcers. Even its deadly fangs had rotted away and dropped out.

Uki's crystal spearhead was lodged in between two of its ribs, sunken deep into the decayed flesh. He tugged hard, dragging it free for another strike, but the snake was too quick.

Even though it had no fangs to bite with, it still had the use of its long, sinuous body. Before Uki could jab it again, the snake wrapped itself around him, squeezing, crushing and lifting him from the ground.

Coils and coils looped across him, slithering tighter and tighter, crushing the air from his lungs. Only the strength of the trapped spirits stopped him from being popped like a fat blister.

Instead he hung there, dangling over the sea of bubbling maggots, his useless spear still clutched in a paw that poked out from the adder's coils. His head jutted out of the top, his eyes still searching the ditch for any sign of his friends.

There was none. Just him, the snake and the muffled sound of crazy, manic laughter.

CHAPTER SIXTEEN

Charice

The snake was slowly suffocating him. Every time he breathed in, it tightened its grip so he had less air in his lungs. If it kept on, he'd soon be out of precious breath.

Uki tried to use all his strength to break its hold, but the beast's scales were like mirrors. His feet slipped off them wherever he tried to find a spot to push against. His arms were pinned to his sides, useless. He sucked in a last gasp, feeling his head begin to spin, the edges of his vision begin to blur.

'Squash, smush, crush, mush, grindy-grind

him into dust.' A sing-song voice echoed around the chamber. The snake turned its head towards it, moving Uki as well. He caught sight of a body emerging from the sea of larvae, like a bather stepping out after a dip.

'Jori ...' he managed to gasp, but it wasn't her. As the maggots and worms fell away, he could see a snakeskin cloak, draped round an old rabbit's body. Her skin, where it wasn't covered in the marks of plague, hung from her bones. Her deep-set eyes were swollen shut and she moved like a puppet being dangled from a string.

'He smells of fire, he does, my children. Burny-burny. Hot orange flames, birdy in the sky with its bright little eye. I spy, I spy, kiss the girls and make them cry.'

'Granny,' Uki tried to shout, but it was an effort to talk. 'Granny Maggitch! If you can hear me ... the creature that's controlling you ... try and fight her off. She's going to kill everyone. All your family, all of the rabbits in the Fenlands ...'

'Who are you talking to, little ball of fluff? Whining like a baby mouse. Squeak, squeak, crunch, die. Soon you'll be just a bump in that snake's tummy. Bumpty dumpty, sat on a wall. Swallowed alive, bones and all . . .'

As Uki stared at the body of Granny Maggitch, jutting out of the pit of larvae, it seemed as though the air around her began to shimmer. Sickly green light swirled, drifting into the shape of Charice.

He had glimpsed her at the Gurdle village, but now he saw her properly. She was tall and skeletal. Her skin was furless and blotched all over with spots and sores. She had tiny ears at the sides of her head, and a strange, pointed nose. The features of an Ancient, like Iffrit and Gaunch.

Long, thin, straggly hair hung from her head, swirling and swaying as if she was floating underwater. Around her neck was a garland of flowers that seemed to be continually growing – blooming, shrivelling and then bursting open again. Except they didn't look like they had petals. They were living, twitching, swelling things – writhing, dividing and spreading.

Diseases, Uki thought. *She's wearing a necklace of diseases.*

She smiled as she spoke to him in her lullaby voice, but it wasn't a nice smile. Wide and manic, showing narrow yellow teeth and blackened gums. It was the grin of someone whose mind has been boiled soft as mashed turnips.

'Charice, please,' Uki said. 'You can take me, but let my friends go . . .'

At the mention of her name, the ancient spirit's face changed. The crazed grin widened and her blank yellow eyes grew tiny pinprick pupils.

'What nom-noms has my petty-pet got here?' she said, as if seeing him for the first time. 'That creeping, crawling *thing* with the fire guardian in his brain? Burning, boiling, trouble and toiling? The snatching sneaker who snaffled my brothers? Got your crystals back, did you? Your brightly blinking baubles? And brought a bunch of thugs to try and burn my creatures . . . my bearers of beautiful blessings . . .'

'They aren't blessings,' Uki tried to shout. 'They're poison! They're going to kill every living creature in the Fenlands!'

'Oh yes, yes, yes!' Charice cackled with horrid

laughter. 'That's what I've made them for. Knit one, purl one; spit one, churn one. All those years stuck in that prison ... I brewed up so many vibrant viruses: such gorgeous germs, perfect plagues, sweet, savoury sicknesses. Now I'm going to unleash them all! Everything will rot and bubble! Sing to me, my pretties!'

'You can't do that ...' Uki started to say, but the spirit was lost in a frantic dance above the surface of the maggots, singing and twirling.

'Hubble, bubble, pus and rubble,' she cooed. 'Down with their buildings, their roads, their meddlings! Atishoo! Atishoo! A plague a day rots the doctor away ...'

'Charice!' Uki shouted, straining against the snake's coils for enough room to snatch a breath. 'If you spread your diseases everywhere, there'll be nothing left! You'll be all on your own! Think how lonely and empty you'll be ...'

'Own? Alone?' Charice shook her head. Her face turned mean. 'Why would I stop? The ones that made me never will. They are the vilest plague of all. They spread and spread, killing everything they touch.

Greed like an ocean. They have eaten the whole world, covered it in poison and junk. Trashtic plastic. The sea is thick with it. Hot smoke, smoggles and foggles. The air, the sky. There will be no end until *they* are ended. Until I wipe the whole world clean and build it up again with my beautiful bacterium.'

Uki realised she was talking about the Ancients. In her unhinged mind, they were still here, still alive. As if all the millennia she had spent locked away hadn't even happened.

'The Ancients . . . the ones that made you . . . have already gone, Charice! You don't need to wipe them out. There are different creatures living here now. Peaceful, innocent ones . . .'

'Gone?' Charice peered across the room at him. Then she nodded to herself. 'Yes. Of course. Gone. You rabbit-things are here now. But you're almost the same as them, underneath the fur, you know. Hoppity-pop. Like cousins. Brothers and sisters, even.'

'We're not! We're nothing like them! We believe in the Goddess. In the Balance! We want to live in harmony with life, not destroy it!'

'Really? Is that so?' Charice moved closer and Uki could see the spindly figure of Granny Maggitch, suspended inside the cloud of green light. 'Liar, liar, world on fire. I *know* that's not true. You're all digging, digging, digging away. In the city ... Eisenfell ... there are metal machines and smoke. The process has already started. Gobble, gobble, gobble. Before long you'll be tearing up the forests, pouring sludge into the sea ...'

'We won't!' Uki shouted. 'I promise!'

'Coughing clouds into the sky, cracking up the bones of the Earth to suck out the marrow, burning, smashing, looting, eating ...'

'That's not true!'

Charice let out a mad, cackling laugh before vanishing back inside the body of Granny Maggitch, who was holding something up between the thumb and finger of one paw. Some kind of wriggling, spiky insect. 'Fiddlesticks and candlewicks. It doesn't matter to me. All this time, all these ages ... I have been practising and perfecting. I have been mixing and meddling. I have been trying to brew, to breed the perfect plague ... the life-ender, the slate-wiper, the begin-againer . . . and I have finally succeeded!'

'What . . . what is that?' Uki asked.

'This? This is a . . . glimpse? A quince? No . . . a nymph! And in it sleeps the seed of a dragonfly. A dream of wings. A hint of a fly. And in the fly curls a virus. And in the virus hides death of everything. Peek-a-boo! I'll kill you! Mammal, bird, fish, insect . . . once this little precious hatches, they will all come tumbling down!'

'No!' Uki kicked and wriggled against the snake, but the thing wouldn't budge. 'You can't do that! Please!'

'Too late, too late. You're going to die now, after a little bit of crunching and swallowing. Snicker-snack, gulp, gulp, burp. And when my dragonfly hatches, everything else will die too!'

Charice began to sing again, snippets of jumbled rhymes and lullabies. She waved her deadly nymph in the air, as if it were a prize, cooing to her snake as it squeezed its coils ever tighter.

Uki could feel his ribs straining, bending inwards. Sparks danced before his eyes. As the snake bent down towards its mistress, he saw the seething pool of larvae below him, squirming away. Would his dead body be dropped in there for them to eat? Or would the snake just swallow him whole?

Jori ... Kree ... Uki sent out his thoughts, unable to spare any more breath to speak. They had come so close ... but for it to end like this ... All Uki could think was how unfair it was.

The larvae seemed to be wiggling faster as he dipped towards them. A million, million tiny mouths with pincers chomping, swimming closer, closer ...

CHAPTER SEVENTEEN

The Lady of the Maggot Lake

A paw.

Uki was wobbling on the very edge of consciousness now, not sure if what he thought he saw was truly there. But there was indeed a paw. And it had a sword.

Like something from one of the legends his mother used to tell, it came up from beneath the surface of the water. Rising slowly, light glimmering along the blade. *A magic blade for the king*, Uki remembered. *Clutched in the paw of a goddess.*

Except this sword wasn't magic. And it wasn't

emerging from a sacred lake. It was Jori's blade, clutched in the tiny hand of Kree, rising up from the disgusting mass of larvae.

Uki could see Kree's beaded leather sleeve with its stripes of red paint. He could see the ripples of dark steel on Jori's Damascus blade. The finely ground edge, like a slice of moonlight.

His friends – they were still alive. The realisation hit him: Charice's diseases couldn't kill them, not with Uki's blood still in their veins, and she had let them slip from her attention. The pulsing waves of sickness she created had ebbed away, giving them the chance to help him.

Uki fought against the blackout that was creeping up on him. He watched Jori's sword draw closer to the snake's body. He had to stay awake, he had to be ready.

Iffrit, give me strength, he prayed to whatever was left of the spirit in his blood. *Gaunch and Valkus, even. For Charice will wipe you out too.*

He wasn't sure if it was his imagination, but he felt a small swell of power. One last scrap, but it was enough for him to tighten his grip on his spear, snagging it tight just before it dropped from his fingers. He craned his head to track the body of Granny Maggitch as Charice made it dance, out of the larvae now and on to the earthen island in the middle of the chamber.

You're only going to have one chance, his dark voice told him. **Don't mess it up.**

And then, in an instant, in half a heartbeat, everything happened at once.

Kree's paw came swiping down, plunging the sword deep into the snake, slicing through buttery flesh and crumbling bone.

The giant serpent flinched in shock – a spasm that made it uncoil like a pent-up spring, shooting Uki upwards into the air, the tips of his ears brushing the earthen ceiling.

From up there, he had a view of the whole chamber. The ring of seething larvae; the collapsing, dying snake; the circular island in the middle, and upon it the tottering, dancing figure of Granny Maggitch, fingers still clutching her precious dragonfly nymph.

Uki didn't pause. Not for a breath.

Even as his little body was fired upwards, he was drawing back his arm, angling the crystal point of his spear down to where Charice was standing.

He pulled together every last scrap of his strength and channelled it into a mighty throw, sending the spear streaming down towards its target, so fast it turned into a streak of white light.

The body of Granny Maggitch had paused in its dance and was just turning to look at the dying snake when the spear struck. Charice hadn't even noticed Uki, who was now tumbling back down from the chamber roof.

Shunk!

The spear hit her in the shoulder, piercing through her tattered snakeskin cloak. As Uki landed in the larvae with a sickening *splat* he looked up in time to see Charice's face appear. The madness, the grin – it had vanished, replaced by a look of stunned horror. She stared at the spear for a moment and then was gone ... sucked down into the crystal along with every last scrap of her aura. All the sickness that had choked the Fenlands ... it swirled round and round like a hurricane, vanishing into the depths of the crystal, into the tiny, tiny realm inside where it would be trapped, this time, forever.

The sensation was like a fever breaking, like a sudden breeze of fresh sea air on a hot afternoon. A nagging sore tooth being pulled, leaving instant pain-free calm in its wake.

The past days had been a constant struggle against Charice's presence, Uki realised. So subtle, he hadn't even sensed it, not until it was gone. He could almost feel every living thing in the Fenlands sigh with relief.

But the crystal needed to be sealed.

Uki began to struggle through the larvae, striking out with his arms and kicking his legs as if he were swimming in a pond. A wriggling, squirming pond that shuddered and jiggled all around him.

A few strokes and he was at the island, hauling himself out. Granny Maggitch had collapsed, the spear still jutting from her shoulder, and he scrambled over to her.

She was barely breathing. Without the presence of Charice possessing her, the plague was starting to eat her frail body alive. Uki had to act quickly.

He grabbed the spear, feeling terrible that it had actually cut into her. Luckily, it was just her shoulder, but perhaps he shouldn't have thrown it so hard? He grabbed her arm with one paw and the spear haft with the other and pulled.

Granny Maggitch's body was very old, her muscles like stringy wire. The spear came out easily and Uki was relieved to see the wound wasn't deep. He would tend to it later. As quickly as he could, he unscrewed the crystal from the haft and slotted it into his harness.

Just like before, he could feel the orange light that was Iffrit's binding power flow out from his body, enveloping the new crystal. He felt the same electric charge of energy as Charice's power became his own. But somehow it was different this time.

The other spirits had given Uki immense strength, speed and healing. Charice's green glow brought him something else. It was a new kind of sense – a connection – joining him to all the living things around him. Similar to when he had first entered the fen and become aware of the teeming life everywhere, but much more intense. It was like he could pick out every single creature – all the countless grubs and maggots, the larger forms of Jori, Kree and Granny Maggitch – he could see their life force in his mind. He could feel the energies coursing through them, he knew how each cell in their body was knitted to the others, how every part of them should feed and shape and work with the rest.

There was a noise at the edge of the earthen platform and he looked up to see Kree clambering out of the larvae, dragging Jori up by her arm. She pulled the larger rabbit safely clear and then did a funny little dance, shaking all the squirming grubs from her body and out of her clothes.

'*Ukku neekneek bulbu bu!*' she shouted. 'That is the most *disgusting* thing that has ever happened to me!'

Uki wanted to rush over to them, but he could *feel* that something was not right with Jori. When he looked at her with his new sight, he could see the toll that her dusk potion had taken. All her energy had burned away, her every muscle had been strained and pulled to the utmost limit. Her brain was thumping with the exertion of driving everything at extra speed, her heart was sore from pounding blood around her system.

Uki closed his eyes and focused on his friend. He spoke to the hurting parts of her body and told them to fix themselves. Instead of using Charice's power to send flowering packages of germs bubbling through her blood, he soothed and healed. He lent some of his strength to her gut, helping it draw energy from the food there. He sent that speeding around her system, giving it power to knit and mend. He calmed the parts of her brain that were blazing with alarms, taking away all the pain she felt. He put all the pieces back into their correct Jori-places, as best he could. Some of the fixing would take more time, he could see, but her body was young and strong. She would be fine.

'What ... what did you do?' Jori was looking up at him, eyes wide, jaw open. 'I could feel you taking it away ... all the sickness from the potion. It's gone ...'

'It's Charice's power,' Uki said. 'I ... I could see what was wrong with you ... and then I made it better.'

'Now *that* is a good power to have!' Kree laughed

and did another little dance. Uki ran over to her then, and grabbed her in a hug. They tumbled to the ground and hugged Jori too, squeezing each other tight with the pleasure of being safe and alive.

'How did you manage to stab the snake?' Uki asked when they finally untangled themselves. 'I thought the maggots had eaten you.'

'They tried to,' said Jori, cringing. 'They were everywhere. And I felt so sick, I could barely move. Then when Charice started talking to you, it eased off. I managed to get my nose above the surface – I could just touch the bottom with my toes – and I could see what was going on.'

'But wasn't it Kree who had the sword?' Uki asked.

'Yes. I could feel something thrashing away nearby. I managed to get over to it, and it was Kree. We kept our heads just under the surface and came up with a plan.'

'It was my idea, actually,' said Kree. 'I climbed on Jori's shoulders, and she walked along the bottom. Then I chopped that huge creature with the sword . . . *swish!* I was amazing, wasn't I?'

'My sword!' Jori sat up, looking around for her precious weapon. Fortunately, it was still jutting out of the snake's side. The enormous adder had collapsed when Charice was captured and was now lying lifeless, half buried in larvae. The diseases in its body had completely taken hold and its flesh was dissolving like ice in the midday sun.

As Jori went to retrieve her blade, Uki remembered Granny Maggitch and ran over to her, peeling her tattered cloak aside to see if there was anything he could do.

She was barely alive. Uki put a paw to her head and drew on his new power, but was horrified to see the damage Charice had done. Every part of the old rabbit was riddled with some kind of sickness. Through and through, down to her bones.

'Jori, hold out your sword,' he said. With a worried look on her face, she did as he asked, but Uki had no intention of harming Granny Maggitch. Instead, he pricked his thumb on the blade and squeezed out a drop of blood, just as he had done with the Gurdles. He gently opened the old rabbit's mouth and let it fall on her tongue.

'I don't know if it will be enough,' he said. 'But with the help of Charice's power, I might be able to save her.'

'I'll carry her outside,' said Jori. 'I can't believe I feel strong enough after taking that much dusk potion, but I think I can manage it.'

Uki nodded, lifting Granny Maggitch up and passing her to Jori. They turned to look at the sea of larvae between them and the chamber door.

'I am *not* going back through that,' said Kree.

'I don't think you'll have to,' said Uki. He closed his eyes and opened his senses to the teeming sparks of life in the ditch. They were all *wrong* somehow. The simple creatures that Charice had rebuilt into new, toxic forms, their only purpose being to deliver her carefully crafted diseases. He could feel their pain, their anguish at every part of themselves being twisted in ways they shouldn't be. Even though they were basically just mouths connected to stomachs, they knew there was a problem. They could sense their bodies weren't assembled properly and it was causing them distress. But it was Charice's will that held them together, that kept their mutated forms from collapsing. A will that was now Uki's.

Rest, he told them. *Let go. You are free now.*

One by one, he released them. He sent his new power coursing through the ditch, taking away all the corruption and damage that Charice had caused. The little larvae blinked out in their hundreds of thousands, their frantic wriggling gradually ceasing. Further still, he reached out across the marshes, the lakes, the rivers – the entire Fenlands – seeking out the creatures who had fallen to Charice's diseases. He made the viruses turn on themselves, burning out and devouring each other. He freed their hosts, curing and healing some, allowing others to sink slowly to the marsh bottom, where their bodies would become food. The process of mending and recovery had begun. With time and growth, he knew, all trace of the evil ancient spirit would be wiped away.

Back in Granny Maggitch's chamber, the ditch was still. The surface level of the larvae sank down as the little grubs perished and dissolved, leaving a shallow pool of filthy swamp water in the bottom. The hunks of meat and bone they had been eating jutted up here and there like the hulls of wrecked ships.

'I'm *still* not walking through that,' said Kree. 'Not even with galoshes on.'

In the end, they used the wooden chair like a stepping stone, throwing it into the ditch, and then leaping on to it from the island, then off again to larvae-free ground. Uki was last to jump, but before he did he paused, looking back down at the spot where Granny Maggitch had lain.

There, where it had been dropped, was Charice's last creation. The dragonfly nymph with the life-ending plague brewing inside. Its six spindly legs were still working as it tried to drag itself across the floor. Its spiky, plated body twitched, bloated with evil poison.

Once more, Uki closed his eyes and focused his new power on it, sensing the poisonous life force within. He could pick out which parts of the soupy goo would twist its eyes, wings, legs and organs. He could *see* the invisibly small particles that would explode into plague when they touched another living body.

Slowly, taking great care to be thorough, he pulled apart the virus piece by tiny piece. He unmade it so thoroughly, there was no trace it had ever existed. Then he brought his booted paw down on top of the nymph, grinding it into the dirt.

With the final, soft *pop* of the undone creature, he thought he could feel the new crystal on his chest buckle twitch. Charice's life's work, her reason for existing, had just been wiped out.

Uki smiled to himself as he followed his friends out of the chamber.

Chapter Eighteen

Healing

Stepping out into the night air, they could feel Charice's absence even more strongly. Everything seemed fresh and new. The whole fen was a healed patient, the morning after a long, painful illness.

'*Neek neek!*' Mooka was still tied in place by the hut door. He jumped up and down in pleasure when he saw them, nuzzling Kree with his pink nose. Jori set about placing Granny Maggitch on his back, using the reins to tie her in place.

'Where's Coal?' Uki said, peering around the

dark camp. There were moving flashes of light at the bottom of the hill, where the Gurdles and Maggitches had been battling, but the top of the mound seemed deserted.

'Maybe he went down to join the fighting,' suggested Kree.

'Maybe he got hurt,' said Uki. 'I'd better try and find him.'

Uki set off at a jog, in and out of the huts and bushes. He half expected to find Coal lying wounded somewhere, a thought that deeply upset him, and so was very relieved when he spotted a figure in the gloom. By the way it leaned on the crutch at its side, it couldn't be anyone else but the one-legged smith. He was standing by the pit that Uki had been trapped in, staring down at the bottom.

'Coal?' Uki called as he drew closer. 'Are you all right?'

Coal looked up, the frown on his face melting into a smile as he recognised Uki. 'Well, bless my ears! You did it!' He reached out to clasp wrists with Uki and gave his arm a squeeze. 'I could feel it, you know. It was like something had been crushing me all these past weeks, and then it was suddenly lifted.'

'Yes, I got her,' Uki said, tapping the green crystal on his harness. 'What are you doing here?'

'Oh,' said Coal, looking back into the hole. 'I got my breath back, you see, and then I was just standing around. I remember you said about those rabbits in the pit that were going to hurt you . . . so I thought I'd see for myself. Teach them a lesson maybe.'

The pit was dark as pitch, but Uki could see that the wooden grille had been lifted off. A fresh trail of torn-up mud led from the far edge, off down the mound.

'They've escaped,' Uki said.

'It would seem so.'

Uki looked out over the dark fen, imagining Necripha and Balto splashing their way back to dry land. He thought he could feel her again ... that spiky purple squiggle of hatefulness. She would soon find more of her Endwatch and be after him once again. Or racing him to find Mortix. Either way, it was a fresh worry, spoiling the sweet feeling of victory he had been enjoying.

Maybe I shouldn't have helped her after all, he thought. But it was done now. He would just have to face what happened.

'Are the others safe?' Coal asked. He was looking out at the marshes too, his deep frown back again. Uki wondered what his thoughts were, why he had really come here, to this empty hole in the ground.

'Yes,' he said. 'They're waiting for us. We should go down and see what's happened to the Gurdles.'

*

There was a strange scene awaiting them at the bottom of Gollop's Mound. All the lanterns the Maggitches had been carrying were now hung from trees and bushes, bathing everything in overlapping pools of orange light.

The Gurdle warriors were standing around, chatting and twirling their weapons, while every single Maggitch lay motionless on the floor.

'Have they killed them all?' Kree asked, as they walked the last few steps down the hill.

'No, I don't think so.' Uki could pick up faint traces of life from the Maggitches, but just like their leader they were now very sick. Charice's plague was racing through their bodies, unchecked.

'Did you break the curse?' Ma Gurdle called out to them as they arrived. She was leaning on a spear for support but still looked fierce in her heron-feather cloak and suit of frogskin armour.

'We did,' said Jori. 'There will be no more sickness in the Fenlands, thanks to Uki.'

There was a cheer from all the Gurdles, cut short by Ma pointing at Granny Maggitch, who was still draped over Mooka's saddle.

'What do *she* be doing there?'

'She's very sick,' said Uki. 'I need to heal her. I need to heal all of these rabbits.'

'*Heal?*' Ma Gurdle almost screamed the word. 'But they's Maggitches! They's the ones that brought this whole curse down on us!'

'It wasn't them,' said Uki. He pointed to the green-glowing crystal on his chest. 'It was the evil spirit, Charice. She's the thing I told you about – the one who was making all the sickness. She took over these rabbits. She made them do her will, but that's finished now. I've trapped her inside this gem.

But without her control, the plague she gave to the Maggitches will kill them.'

'So? They's Maggitches. Let them die.' Ma Gurdle spat on the ground and one or two of her warriors copied her.

'I can't do that,' said Uki, his voice quiet but stern. 'And I don't think you can either. I know you have a feud with them, but would you really leave them to die like this? Don't you remember when you were sick? No rabbit should have to feel that way. No matter what they've done. And whatever happened between your families – you need to put it aside. Set it down. That's what I did, when I felt hatred for what was done to me. It was like giving up a terrible burden. Like being set free.'

Ma Gurdle's icy glare seemed to falter a little. She looked again at the stricken rabbits, lying curled in pain all over the ground.

'This quarrel you have,' Uki continued. 'Can any of you even remember what it was all about?'

There was a lot of mumbling from the Gurdles, most of whom suddenly became very interested in the grass and shrubs at their feet.

'So, why don't you help me bring these sick rabbits back to your village?' Uki said. 'Why don't you let me cure them and help me feed them? Then, when they're better, I bet they won't even want to fight you any more. Maybe then you can all be friends.'

It was the longest speech he'd ever made in front of a group. He was amazed that they seemed to be listening, but also very relieved when Jori stepped in to help him.

'I think,' she said, 'if you give them a chance, you'll find you have more in common than you think. Aren't you all enemies of the Shrikes?'

'Glommating redshells,' said Rawnie.

'Gurt wazzock Spikers,' added Yurdle.

'And you have things like adders and floods and everything else to worry about,' said Uki. 'At the very least you should try to help your neighbours.'

Maybe it was the sudden good feeling caused by the disappearance of Charice. Perhaps it was sympathy after having suffered a dose of the plague themselves. Or it might have been because Uki was the one asking. Lord Maggety-Pie. The rabbit who had brought them back from death.

Whatever the reason, Ma Gurdle's face began to soften. That steely gaze of unbreakable hatred melted – just a fraction at first – and she began to nod her head.

'Very well,' she said. 'Let us show these Maggitches that Gurdles have true hearts. Fix up some stretchers from these here saplings and let's take them all home.'

Uki clapped his paws together and beamed at the heron-cloaked elder, but she flashed him a glare with the last embers of her age-old bitterness.

'Mark you this, though,' she said. 'If just one of them Maggitches wakes up and puts a paw out of place . . .'

'There'll be a muckle gurt reckoning?' Uki suggested.

'Aye, there will,' said Ma Gurdle, the corner of her mouth twitching into a smile. 'Muckle gurt.'

*

It took almost a week for the Maggitches to recover, and there were several that never woke up from the plague.

As soon as they returned to the village, Uki gave

them all a dose of his blood, and then spent every moment he could using Charice's power to try and fix their bodies. The Gurdles helped by making them all comfortable in Ma's longhouse, and by feeding everyone with a constant stream of broth.

Finally, one or two began to stir, to sit, to speak. At first, they were horrified to be in the lair of their hated enemies, but once they realised how they had been saved, their attitudes began to change. Nods came first, then smiles and thanks. By the end, Maggitches and Gurdles were freely chatting with each other. Forming friendships, even. Uki overheard several saying how they didn't know what they had been fighting about in the first place.

Granny Maggitch, against all expectations, recovered quicker than the rest. The wound in her shoulder knitted itself back together without even leaving a scar. She turned out to be a tough old coot, as stubborn as she was wiry. But she, more than all the rest, understood what Uki had done for them. Mainly because she had been aware of all that Charice was plotting, right from the start.

'I was still in there,' she told Uki one morning,

as he fed her broth and worked his healing. 'Tucked away, I was, like a minkle hoppet 'neath a puckstole. I could see all 'twere going on, but I couldn't do one single thing to stop her.'

'It must have been horrible,' said Uki.

'Oh, 'twere.' Granny wiped a tear from her eye. ''Speshully when she brought us to this here village. When she sent out all them poison zimzimmers everywhere and tried to kill all the Gurdles. Gollop knows we've had our differences in the past, but I would never have wished any of 'em dead. Not never.'

Uki gently patted one of her wrinkled paws. It must have been a terrible experience, to be held prisoner in your own mind. And it could easily have happened to him as well – if Iffrit had decided to take control of him, rather than letting himself melt away, giving Uki all his powers. A choice that meant Iffrit could never come back, not according to Necripha. He had literally given up his life for Uki's.

'I promise,' said Granny, breaking Uki's train of thought. 'I promise never to quarrel with them Gurdles again. Life's too short and spiky for that kind of wazzockry.'

'It certainly is,' said Uki, thinking of his mother, of Iffrit, of Nurg's poor brothers. Of all the rabbits who had gone so that he could be here. So that he could stop the ancient spirits before they worked their evil on the world.

*

Not only was she as good as her word, Granny Maggitch even began to form a friendship with Ma Gurdle. Often, when Uki came to check on his patient, he would find her sitting up in bed, chatting away with Ma like old neighbours.

On the day that the healed Maggitches were set to leave, Uki walked into the longhouse to find them both there, waiting for him. Ma's giant frog had returned and it sat between them, its pink tongue licking at its gold-flecked eyes again.

'Good morning, Lord Maggety-Pie,' said Ma with a twinkling smile.

'I wish you wouldn't call me that,' said Uki. 'I'm not a lord of anything.'

'You are to us,' said Granny.

'We've told you many times how muckle grateful we are,' said Ma.

'I know. You don't have to keep saying it.' Uki found himself blushing again.

'Well,' said Ma. 'We figured you and your friends would be wanting to move on, now that the Maggitches is all better.' Uki nodded. He had been talking about it just that morning with Jori.

'We'll be sad to see you go,' said Granny. 'And we wanted to give you something to remember us by.'

She reached down beside her bed and brought out a package, which Uki carefully unwrapped. It was a fine cloak, made from stitched squares of frog and snakeskin. A mixture of the styles worn by the Gurdles and Maggitches. It was lined with soft wool and had a clasp of bronze and silver, decorated with a heron and a frog.

'Lord Bandylegs and Gollop,' said Ma. 'To watch over you in your travels.'

'I . . . I don't know what to say . . .' Uki stroked the delicate stitching. 'It's beautiful.'

He had managed to scrub the mud out of his clothes and patch their holes, but his cloak still lay in one of the mound's chambers, ripped to shreds.

As much as he missed it, it was nowhere near as fine as this one.

'You'll always find a welcome here in the Fenlands,' said Granny.

'That you will,' agreed Ma. 'And if there's anything else we can do to help . . .'

'Actually,' said Uki, 'there is.'

He told them about his plan to go south, following the distant call of Mortix, the last spirit. They offered to take him and his friends as far as the edge of the fen, to a town called Enk.

'We don't go in the town itself,' said Granny. 'Happen it be full of Spikers. But we do have friends and customers there. We'll get someone to sneak you out, on to the southern road.'

The rest of that day was spent preparing to leave. The Maggitches were saying their goodbyes, and the Gurdles were getting ready to break up the village. They had stayed in one place much longer than they usually liked to and were worried about Shrikes finding them.

Uki, Jori and Kree went about saying their farewells. Little Bo was especially sad to see them go. He gifted Kree a dagger made from an adder's fang, and Jori a bone set of the board game the Gurdles liked to play: 'hoppet and snapsters'.

Just as they were getting themselves ready for Ma Gurdle's raft to be cast off, Coal came over to them.

'I hear tell you're heading south,' he said.

'We are,' said Uki. 'Although I don't know where exactly. I can just feel the last spirit is in that direction.'

'Well,' said Coal. 'I happen to be from down that way. If you still need a guide ... or maybe a friend ...'

'Are you trying to go with us?' Kree asked. 'Why don't you just come out and say it?'

'He's trying to be tactful, Kree,' said Jori. 'Something you know absolutely nothing about. But I'd like to know his reasons for asking, even so.'

Coal nodded, then scratched at his scarred chin, trying to find the right words.

'I don't really have a proper reason,' he said finally. 'Just that I have seen amazing things I'd never thought possible. When my accident happened, I thought my life was over. That I'd never be useful again. Now I know the quest you are all on … how important it is … and I'd like to help. So I can feel as if I have a purpose once more. Does that make sense?'

Uki gave a little hop. 'Of course it does! I'd love it if you came. We all would, wouldn't we?'

'Yes,' said Kree. 'His ugly face will help scare off bandits.' She laughed as Coal pretended to swipe at her with his hammer. Uki looked at Jori, whose ears were twitching in thought.

'I suppose a guide will be useful,' she said. 'And he does know how to look after himself.'

'*Neek!*' Mooka hopped over and gave Coal's arm a nuzzle.

'Then come along I will,' he said. 'Truth be told, I'll be glad to have solid earth under my paws again. I've been in these marshes far too long.'

Uki agreed with him. He had taken off his horrid galoshes and was looking forward to feeling grass and daisies beneath his toes.

They all stood at the bow of Ma Gurdle's raft as the ropes between the vessels were untied. Gradually, one by one, the boats split off and slid out of the lake in different directions, disappearing down channels and streams amongst the reeds, charting separate, secret paths to the next location of the floating village.

When only the huge longhouse raft and Rawnie's dinghy were left, they sailed out from under the sweeping willow branches, catkins pattering around them like snow, and set off down the river, a fresh marsh breeze rustling the reeds beside them.

Uki's fingers played over the buckle on his chest, counting the crystals that held the spirits he and his friends had captured and brushing the empty hole that would contain the last.

Mortix. The spirit of death.

Every bone in his body, every memory Iffrit had shared with him, told him she would be the most dangerous, the hardest yet. But if you had said a few days ago, when everything seemed lost, that he would save his companions and heal the swamp, he wouldn't have believed it.

We'll do it, he thought to himself. *Somehow. As long as we're together. Nothing can stop us.*

Jori, standing next to him, caught his eye and

twitched an ear at the hopeful expression on his face. Without knowing why, Uki found himself beaming back at her, then at Kree, who gave a giggle. Soon, all three were chuckling out loud, holding their sides, eyes full of happy tears and the joy of being safe and free.

Look at you, said his dark voice. **Laughing in the face of Death.**

I am, Uki agreed. *I quite literally am.*

CHAPTER NINETEEN

The Rescue

T he bard stops and bows his head slightly. A signal that the story is finished. Rue jumps to his feet and applauds, while Jori is silent. She turns her head to look out through the hole in the rubble, trying to hide the tears in her eyes.

'I knew they would beat Charice!' Rue says, hopping from leg to leg. 'And Necripha, too!'

'I'm glad you're enjoying this story as much as Podkin's,' says the bard, reaching for the water flask to wet his dry lips.

'And what about the Maggitches and the Gurdles?

Did they stay friends? Did Uki go back and visit them again?'

The bard rolls his eyes. 'One story at a time,' he says. 'Let's save that one for the next time we're trapped in a tower by evil cultists.'

Rue nods, then takes his place by the fire again. He casts a few glances over at Jori, as if working up the nerve to say something.

'Is that it?' asks the bard. 'Nothing more to ask? You normally give me earache with all your jabbering, once a story is finished.'

There is something Rue would like to ask, but it's a question for Jori, not the bard. A personal question he has a feeling she might not like. He wants to know what happened to Uki and Kree. Why she is here in the tower and they are not. Did they die during the tale? Are they still around somewhere in Hulstland? Will one of them appear in real life at any minute?

But something about the fierce warrior stops the questions before they bubble out of his mouth. She is not like the bard, whose grumpiness is mostly pretend (at least, Rue hopes it is). No, he has a feeling that – as kind as Jori has been to him – she is someone who needs to be treated carefully. Someone who, if you ever got on the wrong side of them, might never speak to you again. And besides, it's not a good idea to offend a rabbit with a very sharp sword. Especially one who could shred your ears into ribbons in the space of a blink.

'What did you think, Jori?' the bard says, his voice gentle. 'Did I do it justice?'

Jori is silent for a moment more, then she wipes her eyes and turns back to them. 'You did,' she says. 'I never knew some parts of the story. How scared Uki was when we were all sick. How alone he must have felt. And there was much I had forgotten. Like our stay with Father Klepper. Those were happy days. Our little family . . .'

She drifts off again and Rue decides that it's now or never. If he asks really, *really* nicely, she might tell him what happened to Uki.

He is just clearing his throat to speak, when there is a noise from outside. A shout that echoes about the old ruins.

'*Nyath n'kaaaaa!*'

Jori and the bard both leap to their feet and rush

to the hole in the rubble, staring out.

'That was an Arukh war cry!' says the bard. 'Is it a raiding party from the mountains?'

'No.' Jori points. 'It's just a single rabbit. He's got a sword and leather armour. He doesn't look like an Arukh brave. Could it be . . . ?'

'Jaxom!' shouts the bard. 'They're here! They got the message!'

Rue cranes his neck to see and gets a glimpse of Jaxom charging through the ruins, yelling. A cloaked Endwatch rabbit is perched on top of an old wall, firing black-feathered arrows at him. He dodges one, knocks a second aside with his sword, and then another arrow – bright red – flies in return to hit the Endwatcher, toppling him from his perch.

'Nikku is there as well!' says the bard. 'I recognise her scarlet fletchings.'

'I'd better help them,' says Jori. 'While the Endwatch are distracted. You two stay here, where it's safe.'

She unclips her flask and takes a sip of dusk potion, then scrambles out of the rubble-hole and charges into the fray, her sword swishing circles through the air.

Rue watches her go. His little heart is pounding in his chest, his whole body jangles with a mixture of terror and excitement. Part of him feels like burrowing under the bard's cloak until all the fighting is done, but another realises he is going to miss the whole thing, stuck cowering in the tower.

This could be my first story, he thinks. *My first tale. A clash between good and evil, and I was there to see it!*

In his mind he sees himself on the stage at the Festival of Bards, telling a hushed audience all about the way a dusk wraith moves in battle. How arrows sound when they *zip* past your head. *The Victory of the Foxguard*, he will call it.

Before he really knows what he is doing, he darts out of the hole after Jori.

'Rue, no!' the bard shouts behind him and his paw clutches at Rue's cloak, but the little rabbit is too quick. He slithers down the mound of rubble outside the door and runs into the ruins, following the sound of fighting.

There are more war cries, yells of pain and the sound of metal striking metal.

Just behind that wall, Rue thinks, and he clambers up the blackened brickwork of what might once have been a house.

Looking down, he spots Jori locked in combat with an Endwatch rabbit. Her sword is moving too fast to even see, forcing the Endwatcher backwards until his blade clatters out of his hands and Jori clouts him on the head.

Off to his left, Jaxom is fighting another, striking with his sword, kicking out with his feet. There is one more black-cloaked figure, tumbled at the foot of a crumbling wall, a red-fletched arrow jutting from its arm.

Is it dead? Rue wonders in horror. He has never seen a dead rabbit before. He has never seen such violence. He thought it would be exciting, but it isn't. It's brutal and scary and he suddenly wants to be with the bard again, safe in the tower.

'Rue! Get down from there!' He hears the bard's voice from somewhere behind him and is about to turn around when the fallen Endwatch rabbit moves. There is a *twang* and something punches him in the chest, knocking him backwards off the wall. He feels

himself falling, falling, and then the ground hits him from behind. He is lying on stones, on rocks, and there is something sticking out of his body. Long and thin with a tuft of black on the end. Is it a flower? Why is it making his chest burn? Why is everything turning wobbly?

Rue looks up and sees the sky beginning to circle around his head, spinning, spinning. The bard's face appears, but it's all stretchy and wrong. His voice is blurry and strange, like everything is underwater.

Help me, Rue tries to say, but his mouth won't work properly. His sight is going fuzzy, dark round the edges. The last thing he thinks of is his epic story, the battle he was longing to describe.

I didn't see it all, he thinks. *I don't know how it ends.*

And then he is gone.

'Rue!' the bard screams. 'Rue!'

He is clutching the little rabbit's body, patting at his face, trying to wake him up. He hears a scream from somewhere behind the wall, then another. Feet scrabble amongst the rubble and then Jori is beside him, Jaxom too. A moment later, Nikku appears.

'The little one!' Jaxom shouts, and falls to his knees beside the bard. Jori is bent over, examining the arrow wound.

'Is he breathing?' she asks. Her eyes have begun to droop now the dusk potion has worn off and her body is paying the price. Her paws are starting to tremble, but she is fighting it, desperate to help Rue.

'Yes,' says the bard. 'I think so.'

'The arrow hasn't gone too deep,' says Jaxom. 'His cloak stopped most of it. I think I can pull it out.'

'What about the Endwatch?' Nikku asks. She is standing over them, an arrow fitted to her bow.

'I finished off mine, and the one who shot Rue,' says Jaxom.

'I knocked mine out,' says Jori. 'He won't be moving for a while.'

'I'll make sure,' says Nikku, and disappears before Jori can stop her. Jaxom has hold of the arrow and is about to tug it free.

'Please be careful,' says the bard.

Jaxom nods, then gives the arrow a yank. It comes clear, leaving a small hole in Rue's cloak, just below his left shoulder.

'Only a flesh wound,' says Jaxom. 'Why isn't he awake?'

Jori takes the arrow from him and sniffs the end. It has a long, narrow bodkin point and is smeared with a black substance.

'Poison,' she says. 'Crowsbane, I think. It's found around here. I can make an antidote, but I need purple haircap moss and eagle mushrooms. They grow ... high up in the mountains ...'

Jaxom stands and shouts out across the ruins. 'Search the Endwatchers, Nikku! We need the antidote!'

There is a moment before she returns. 'Nothing on them except some dried turnips,' she says. 'And I've finished off the third one. They'll not trouble us any more.'

'Can you save Rue?' the bard asks Jori. 'Is he going to die?'

She looks up at him, her eyes beginning to drift shut. Each word is an effort for her. 'Depends ... how much ... poison he took. Without ... antidote ... doesn't look good.'

'Curse it!' the bard shouts, tears spilling down his

cheeks. 'I was too slow to stop him! I should never have brought him here in the first place!'

'It's our fault as well,' says Jaxom. 'We should have got here quicker.'

'We rode as fast as we could,' says Nikku. 'But we met another Endwatcher on the path. It took us some time to deal with him.'

'Did you get my message?' the bard asks, remembering why they were here. 'Did you raise the Foxguard? They have to get to Thornwood. As many as possible. The Endwatch will be going after Podkin.'

Nikku nods. 'I travelled to Melt soon after you, and was at Gant's when the sparrow arrived. He has sent out word to every Foxguard in the Five Realms. Podkin will be protected, don't worry.'

As Nikku speaks, Jori reaches across a shaking paw and grabs the bard's cloak.

'I have just thought. There may be hope . . . in the mountains . . . not far from here . . . an Arukh tribe. Uki and I . . . met them once . . .'

'And they'll have the antidote?' The bard grasps Jori, suddenly hopeful.

'They might.' She lets out a groan. 'The ingredients, at least. But we must ... be quick ...'

'I know the tribe she speaks of,' says Jaxom, his face grim. 'They're as likely to skin us as help us.'

'But we have to try,' says the bard. 'I can't let anything happen to Rue. I *can't.*'

'Then we will go,' says Nikku. 'We can ride in Jaxom's cart through the foothills, then continue on foot. Rue is Foxguard now. He must be saved.'

'Thank you,' the bard sobs. Jaxom and Nikku help the staggering Jori stand and begin to limp over to his cart. The bard scoops up the almost lifeless body of Rue and cradles him, one paw keeping pressure on his shoulder wound.

'You're going to be all right, little one,' he whispers. 'By Clarion and the Goddess, you're going to be all right. Please. Get better and you can ask me all the questions in the world. I won't complain once, I promise.'

Carrying him oh so gently, the bard follows the others, out of the foothills and up into the cold stone peaks of the Arukh mountains beyond.

A Glossary of Fenland Dialect

Bollycracker – bottom. Or, if you want to be rude, bum

Chin-waggle – chat

Dilly-version – a diversion, a bluff

Glommating – flipping

Glopstalk – to walk through mud or marsh

Glopstickers – Maggitch warriors who attack from under the mud or water, using primitive breathing masks

Gollop – Fenland god. A giant frog who made the fen and is supposed to live in Toadtwitch Lake

Gurt – great/large

Hoppet – frog

Hopsnatcher – grass snake

Maggety-pie – magpie

Minkle – little

Mollygogglers – children

Muckle – much/big/very

Mudwalker – someone from outside the Fenlands

Nammet – food

Paddlewhack – to hit

Pikenoddling – stupid, unintelligent. Having the brains of a pike

Puckstole – toadstool

Redshell – a member of Clan Shrike

Snaggled – caught/trapped

Snapster – pike

Spiker – a member of Clan Shrike

Wazzock – stupid rabbit

Zaggert – adder

Zimzimmer – dragonfly

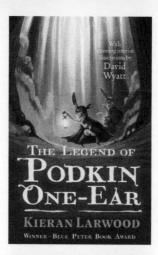

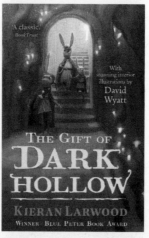

Have you read the other exciting adventures in the Five Realms series?

A thick white blanket covers the wide slopes of the band of hills known as the Razorback Downs . . .

Podkin is the son of a warrior chieftain. He knows that one day it will be up to him to lead his warren and guard it in times of danger. But for now, he's quite happy to laze around annoying his older sister, Paz, and playing with his baby brother, Pook. Then Podkin's home is brutally attacked, and the young rabbits are forced to flee. The terrifying Gorm are on the rampage, and no one and nowhere is safe. With danger all around them, Podkin must protect his family, uncover his destiny, and attempt to defeat the most horrifying enemy rabbitkind has ever known.

Discover Fantastic Faber Reads

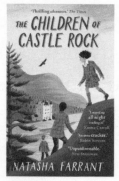

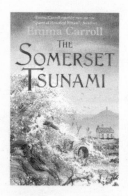